I0651197

Joseph Fitzgerald Molloy

The Most Gorgeous Lady Blessington

Vol. I

Joseph Fitzgerald Molloy

The Most Gorgeous Lady Blessington
Vol. I

ISBN/EAN: 9783743373112

Manufactured in Europe, USA, Canada, Australia, Japa

Cover: Foto ©Raphael Reischuk / pixelio.de

Manufactured and distributed by brebook publishing software (www.brebook.com)

Joseph Fitzgerald Molloy

The Most Gorgeous Lady Blessington

THE MOST GORGEOUS

LADY BLESSINGTON

BY

J. FITZGERALD MOLLOY.

AUTHOR OF

'COURT LIFE BELOW STAIRS,' 'THE LIFE
AND ADVENTURES OF PEG WOFFINGTON,' 'THE LIFE
AND ADVENTURES OF EDMUND KEAN,' 'ROYALTY RESTORED,
OR LONDON UNDER CHARLES II.,' 'FAMOUS PLAYS,' 'THE FAITHS
OF THE PEOPLES,' ETC.

WITH A PORTRAIT OF LADY BLESSINGTON

IN TWO VOLUMES

VOL. I.

DOWNEY & CO.
12 YORK STREET, COVENT GARDEN, LONDON
1896

CONTENTS

CHAPTER I

CHAPTER II

CHAPTER III

CHAPTER IV

CHAPTER V

CHAPTER VI

CHAPTER VII

CHAPTER VIII

CHAPTER IX

PREFACE

STRANGE as the statement may seem, it is not less true that no luminous biography of Lady Blessington has been written: strange because her life presents in itself a romance such as facts seldom contain or combine; such as Fate denies to ordinary mortals.

Virtue and happiness, beautiful and enviable as they are, afford meagre material for memoirs. It is they whose swift - stirred sympathies and longings for happiness carry them beyond the pale of the commonplace and the bonds of conventionality, whose loves are ill-starred and whose lives are shadowed ; they who strive and suffer, who aspire and falter, who possess and present studies that move and fascinate us. Their heart histories appeal from out the past for green places in our memories.

Of such was the gifted and beautiful Irishwoman—'the most gorgeous Lady Blessington' as she was styled by Dr Parr, and as she was known to her intimates—whose biography is here written with an admiration that borders on affection, and with that sympathy which sorrow solicits.

In writing the opening sentence the fact has not been overlooked that some fifty years ago 'A Memoir of the Literary Life and Correspondence of the Countess of Blessington' was written by Dr Madden, who for years had enjoyed her acquaintance, and into whose possession some of her correspondence passed after her death.

The production of this Life of my Lady Blessington is partly due to the fact that the writer has been kindly permitted to make use of the six volumes in Mr Morrison's possession of letters addressed by the leading men and women of the day in literature, art and society to the Countess, or written by herself. Here are published for the first time letters or parts of letters which Disraeli, Dickens, Landor, Barry Cornwall, Marryat, Macready, Lord Lytton and others addressed to her.

The letters given here are not pitchforked into the pages irrespective of what has gone before, or of what remains behind ; but are introduced to illustrate a character, to strengthen statements, occasionally to enlarge a view. Frequently the information contained in the correspondence is embodied in the memoir without reference to their writers, lest such might break the even flow of the narrative.

For much valuable information the writer is likewise indebted to manuscripts found in the archives of the British Museum Library; to biographies, lives, and letters of the contemporaries of the Countess who came within the circle and felt the charm of her influence; and to the verbal descriptions of two friends who knowing her history appreciated her worth.

That the same appreciation and charm may be felt by those who here read this record of Lady Blessington's life, is a satisfaction which the writer wishes to one and all, his critics included.

J. FITZGERALD MOLLOY.

THE MOST GORGEOUS
LADY BLESSINGTON

CHAPTER I

An Irish Squireen—A Sensitive Child—the Joy
of being Understood—Dreams—The Desmonds
Themselves — Wild Times — Rebel Hunting—
Tragedy—A Domestic Tyrant—Suitor's Twain—
Proposals—Forced to Marry—Misery—Frenzy—
Escape—The Prelude of Her Life.

MORE than a century has passed since a child
was born into the world whose strange and
changeful career from its bitter beginning
even to its close, could count as experiences,
reversals of fortune, phases of mystery, in-
felicity [of marriage, and the passion of love ;
these rich elements of romance that lend
fascination to reality. This child, born on
the first day of September 1789 at Knockbrit

near Clonmel in the county of Tipperary in Ireland, was christened Margaret Power. Her father Edmund Power an Irish squireen was the descendant of an ancient family residing in the adjacent county of Waterford ; whilst her mother a County Limerick woman, delighted to trace her descent from Maurice first Earl of ˙ Desmond, and to enumerate for the benefit of her children and her neighbours the great and noble houses with which her family was connected.

Edmund Power was a man whose high spirit not infrequently led him into violence ; whose love of sport caused him to neglect such merely mercenary matters as the cultivation of his property ; whose desire to entertain and whose love of display, drifted him into debt and difficulties, after the fashion of his kind in the days in which he dwelt. Tall straight-built and handsome, florid of face, peremptory of speech, he dressed in leather breeches and top boots, wore white cravats, frills, ruffles, and top seals, which costume helped to ˙ give him a showy and impressive appearance, and to gain for him amongst his fellow squires the names of Beau Power, and Shiver the Frills. His wife whom he had married early in life seems to have been an inactive woman, too weak to influence her husband or avert his ruin ; and too much absorbed in the glories of 'me ancestors the Desmonds' to enter into the inner lives of her children, of whom she bore six.

Margaret the third of these, if not quite overlooked was little cared for in her childhood. Extremely delicate, nervous, and excessively sensitive, she sat apart, silent and pale-faced whilst her robust brothers and sisters romped, played, and teased her for not joining in their sports : she, being all unlike them physically as well as mentally : for whilst they were remarkably handsome, she was considered comparatively plain. During the time she remained apart from their joyous company, her mind—the strange mysterious kingdom of a child's mind, which can only be entered into by those possessing the passport of sympathy—was receiving impressions, thinking out ideas, perceiving facts which when put into words led her nurse to consider her uncanny, perhaps a changling, and confirmed the general impression that one so sad of manner whilst yet so young, so weak in body and with such wistful eyes, could not live long.

With age she gained strength, but her characteristics remained; and the quaint speculative questions she asked, the occasional gleams of insight she showed, the comments she passed, which previously had only excited ridicule, now attracted to the shy child the attention of a friend of the family, Miss Anne Dwyer, a voluble-tongued, kind-hearted woman, with great natural though uncultivated gifts, whose vivacity and repartee led her to be regarded as a person of ability by those incapable of judging her talents. She was sympathetic and clever enough to see that Margaret was in no ways understood by those around her, and generous enough to devote herself to this lonely child in whose nature great qualities possibly lay dormant. Therefore the latter

4

was encouraged to make those inquiries which formerly had produced only laughter, but which now were answered with all the clearness and ability that Anne Dwyer possessed.

The joy which the poor child found in being understood was pathetic; a hand had been held out to her in solitude, to which she eagerly clung, and she was prepared to learn whatever lessons her instructress proposed, and to lay bare her mind to one so capable of satisfying its demands. One day the pupil asked where her teacher had gained her knowledge, and when answered it was from books, Margaret developed a passion for reading which increased with years and continued through life. A faculty she had always possessed now began to show itself, when her vivid imagination conjured up scenes, peoples, and events, at first for the benefit of her brothers and sisters who loved strange tales, but afterwards for the entertainment of her parents' guests; for her father and mother being first astonished, soon grew interested in her powers of story-telling.

Now Edmund Power's property which at one time had brought him fifteen hundred a year, became through neglect and increasing debt of less and less value. But so long as he could have dogs and hunters, and enjoy wine and revelry, the world went well with him and he was content to put off till to-morrow such unpleasant considerations as tradesmen's bills and obtruding bailiffs. The day came however when such sinister sights could no longer be shut out, and he was obliged to leave Knockbrit and take up his residence in Clonmel, when, though retaining some part of his property, he entered into partnership as a corn merchant and butter buyer with Messrs Hunt & O'Brien whose business premises were in the neighbouring city of Waterford.

To the inexperienced change is ever delightful, and the removal of the family was hailed with pleasure by the children with the exception of Margaret, who looked forward with sad foreboding to leaving the place she had peopled with her dreams; the country

with its distant hills on whose blue heights
bonfires flamed against the black on the Eves
of St James and St John ; the far fields where
under the sleeping moonlight, hand in hand
in circles weird, fairies danced around rings,
their sportive figures aerial as the violet shadows
from which they sprang ; the lanes down
which the gracious knight who sought her
all the world o'er, one day would come :
the desolate moors across which the headless
horseman strove to outride the winds on winter
nights ; and the dark river by which the blanch-
robed banshee was seen to walk. None of
these things were to be found in a town whose
streets and shops and peoples were less dear
and sacred to her than the scenes over
which she had roamed uncontrolled, a silent
self-communing child, solitary save for the
luminous dreams that lighted the world
round.

But her feelings on this point as on others
were not entered into by her family, and
stealing from them on the last evening of
their stay under the old home roof, she a

sad and lonely figure moving through the thickening grey, walked to the spots which association and memories had made sweet to her, to bid them all farewell; conscious possibly that some link uniting the past and the future, was being snapped in the chain of her life; a chain which time could never unite, bring the years what they would. On her return, stealthy and timid, she carried with her a few wild flowers for remembrance, and with an intuition which teaches that what is sacred to oneself should be hidden from all, she thrust them into her pocket from which only when alone was she to release and carry them to her lips.

The small and incommodious house into which they moved, stood near an old stone bridge that joined the counties of Clonmel and Waterford, at a place called Suir Island. Here soon after their arrival occurred a little scene which vignette like, illustrates the character of Margaret and the lack of understanding shown by her family. Whilst Mrs Power received some friends who were admiring the other children for their strength and beauty, Margaret who had no share in the general praise stood silently by, eagerly listening, and hardly observed until one of the circle turning towards her said, 'Come here my dear and show me what you have bulging in your pocket.'

Margaret, confused and nervous, refused to stir until her mother beckoned her, when blushing because of the notice she attracted, and fearful of its result, she crossed the room when the contents of her pocket, the flowers she had gathered in Knockbrit were brought to light amidst much laughter, and contemptuously flung out of the window. On this the child burst into a passion of tears she could no longer keep back, when she was sternly reproved for being foolish and ill-tempered.

The change which was made about the year 1797 must have been galling to a poor proud lady who was 'a real descendant of the Desmonds themselves,' as well as to the squireen husband whose ancestors 'had never dirtied their hands by earning a penny piece.' The change however had its compensations, for the business in which he had become a partner prospered greatly, and promised to restore his fortunes and secure independence to his children.

Unhappily this state of affairs did not continue long, for in an evil hour he listened to a proposal, the acceptance of which brought about his ruin. This proposal made by Lord Donoughmore was that Edmund Power should become a magistrate for the counties of Tipperary and Waterford. The social distinction which this situation offered was one to comfort and flatter Beau Power, now lowered in his dignity and wounded in his pride. Once more the squireen might hold his head high, might hunt with and entertain the military and the county families, and become a person to be feared and flattered by the coerced and terror-stricken people. That no salary or other reward was attached to the office seemed no drawback to its acceptance, and was a matter this fine gentleman would regard as beneath his consideration : on the other hand promises were held out by his lordship, then a person of influence at the Castle, of a lucrative post for services rendered the government, and even hints of a baronetcy were not withheld from him. Power gladly accepted the offer though it involved a change of his religion : for he had been born and bred a Catholic and until now had nominally belonged to the church whose members were considered in-eligible for the magistracy. He therefore conformed to the Protestant religion, an act regarded with abhorrence by his family and friends ; and so long and no longer as there remained a chance of his receiving the promised rewards from his patron, did he continue to profess that faith.

To understand the duties a magistrate was then called on to perform, and the manner in which he carried them out, it is necessary to bear in mind the state of the times. Long suffering from distress and discontent, Ireland was now seething with rebellion. The United Irishmen founded by Wolfe Tone in 1791 with the object of forcing the government to relax the terrible severity of the laws which oppressed the people, and if necessary to invite French aid towards helping them to liberty, had become a secret society which numbered half a million members. Not only were their meetings prohibited, but the local magistrates in whose hands the execution of the most vigorous measures were entirely left, were empowered to send all persons suspected of belonging to the movement into the navy : to search houses for arms : and to treat as culprits all who should be absent from their homes without a satisfactory cause after a certain hour in the evening. The magistrates in their search for Insurgents were accompanied by the military who practised horrible outrages ; sometimes, under the pretext that arms were concealed in them, houses were plundered and burned and their inhabitants subjected to torture by way of forcing a confession. In October 1796 the Habeas Corpus Act was suspended; and all Ireland was proclaimed under martial law in March 1798, in which year the rebellion broke out.

A fearless horseman and a determined enemy of rebels, Power rode at night through the terrorised country whose black and mournful silence was broken only by the clattering troop of dragoons following him; seizing upon all chance wayfarers, searching suspected houses, and striking terror into the hearts of peasants in the darkness of their cabins; whilst by day the severity of his punishments caused him to be the dread and the curse of the unfortunate men brought before him. As a consequence the friends of those wronged by his tyranny, burned his corn stores, killed his cattle, and destroyed his crops, and his partners after many attempts, at last succeeded in getting rid of so obnoxious a person. In return for these misfortunes he received letters from the Castle acknowledging his services and praising his zeal, and on presenting himself at the vice-regal court, he was shown gratifying marks of attention, and given fresh promises of reward which might have been kept had not his office, as a magistrate been abruptly ended by an act which throws a lurid light upon these troubled times, and illustrates the character of this man.

It happened one April evening that a young farm labourer, named John Lonnergan, the son of a widow, was in his cabin when he proposed to take to a neighbouring forge a pitchfork which had been broken.

'Johnnie dear it's too late to go' said the widow 'maybe its Power and the soldiers you'd be meeting.'

'Never mind mother' answered the lad 'sure I'll only leave it and hurry back; you know I can't do without it to-morrow;' and away he went light-heartedly to meet his fate.

He had not gone a mile from his home when he caught the quick clatter of hoofs on the narrow road and looking behind saw through the gathering grey of this spring evening, the man who was the terror of the country, riding at a furious rate, and followed by two others. The lad in his fright jumped over a ditch and ran through the adjoining fields, seeing which Power who was probably far from sober, believed he had discovered a rebel, called out to, and then fired at him, when he fell covered with blood. At sound of the report, a woman named Bridget Hannan rushed to the spot where she saw Power standing on a ditch, a smoking gun in his hand, who said he would shoot her if she came any further. Lonnergan who was still living but quite insensible, was taken and flung on horseback behind Power's servant to whom he was strapped, when the party rode into Clonmel and in the first instance turned into the stableyard of the magistrate whose family startled to attention by his oaths, hurried to the windows to 'see a lad apparently dead, his head sunk upon his breast, his clothes steeped with blood, his limbs hanging powerless from the horse on which he was held. In this condition he was taken to the court house or jail where the blood by that time being well nigh drained from his veins, he survived only a few hours; his body smeared and stark, being then hung up for exhibition above the grim gateway of the old stone building, that the people might be warned by the ghastly sight from all tendencies to rebel.

Now the widow having watched through the lonely night for the return of her son, went in the soft flush of early morning to make inquiries for him at the forge, where he had not been seen nor heard of; and from there she walked into Clonmel, anxious and weary, hoping and fearing, but no trace of him could she find until in passing the jail she was attracted by sight of that at which a mournful crowd was silently gazing. One glance told her mother's heart what it was, when with a piercing shriek she fell to the ground. Presently when she recovered consciousness and had learned how it was her 'Johnnie dear' had been taken from her, she knelt upon the rough pavement in front of that ghastly figure, and with all the fervour and eloquence of her race, cursed his murderer.

It is probable that no notice would have been taken of this occurrence, which Power set down to his zeal for the government, if the murdered lad's family had not been urged by their landlord Bagnell, who hated Power because of his alliance with the Donoughmore interest, to prosecute the magistrate. Even when proceedings were taken against him, the grand jury composed of men like himself, threw out the bill, and it was only when a second bill was sent up that it was accepted, and he was returned to take his trial for murder. The defence was that Lonnergan was one of a dangerous gang of rebels, and that he had fired a stone at his murderer, statements for which no evidence was forthcoming. The result was that Power, as an active agent for the government, was acquitted, but that his name was removed from the magistracy.

Previous to his trial he had at Lord Donoughmore's suggestion, and in order to advocate his lordship's political views, become the proprietor of the *Clonmel Gazette* or *Munster Mercury*, the editor of which was Bernard Wright, a wit, a poet, and a teacher of foreign languages, but no politician; who, because a letter in the French language had in 1798 been found upon him, had received a hundred lashes by order of Sir John Judkin

Fitzgerald 'an extremely active, spirited, and meritorious magistrate' as the parliamentary proceedings styled him. Edmund Power knew nothing of newspapers and this venture merely served to sink him deeper in the mire of debt. The state of his finances was such that his daughters, amongst other humiliations, were made to feel that their school fees were unpaid, and were prevented from learning certain kinds of fancy work, without a knowledge of which no girl's education was considered complete.

Laughed at for his pretensions by the class whom he sought, hated as a renegade and an enemy of his country by the class he despised, baffled in his hopes of obtaining recognition and reward from the government he served, he was a soured and a desperate man. Always given to conviviality he now became dissipated, and as a consequence his temper grew more violent, his fits of rage more frequent; he treated his wife with brutality, and became the terror of his home where he delighted to display his tyranny. The slightest disregard to his wishes was punished by flinging knives, plates, cups, or whatever came readiest to his hand, at the heads of the offenders. Terror-stricken by his drunken fury, his cruelty, and his desperate oaths, his children fled from his approach, and as a result of the misery of their home, his eldest daughter Anne fell into a nervous condition which speedily brought about her death.

Notwithstanding the state of his circumstances he continued to entertain recklessly, by way of keeping up appearances; and when in 1803 a regiment of the 47th foot was ordered to Clonmel, he invited the officers to dinner. Amongst those who accepted his invitation were Captain James Murray and Captain Maurice St Leger Farmer, both of whom became ardent admirers of Margaret Power. Though only fourteen years old at this time, she was in the habit of sitting at her father's table when he received company; but it is significant that when these young men came to her home, she, a mere school-girl, was considered too young to be formally introduced to them.

From the fact that their other children possessed more regularity of feature, her parents were not quick to recognise the charm that depended more on colour and expression which Margaret, now the eldest daughter, began to develop. Her large grey-blue eyes, wistful, winsome, and almost dark in the shadow of long lashes, were contrasted by abundant brown hair rather light in colour; her face round and soft, was fresh and clear in complexion with sweet little dimples that lapsed into smiles: her exquisitely shaped head with its tiny pink ears was gracefully poised upon white sloping shoulders, blue veined like her arms: whilst her hands were so beautiful that years later they served as models to Henry Barlowe the sculptor. Her figure gave promise of a grace that already marked her movements; whilst not the least of those charms which were subsequently to exercise forcible influence over others, was her voice, which low, soft, caressing, and just flavoured with an accent that gave it piquancy, fell wooingly upon the ear.

Little wonder that these young men felt the fascination of this girl with her winsome beauty and her child-like shyness; a fascination they lost no time in declaring. Though showing no affection for either, she liked Captain Murray far the better of the two, his frank face, good humour, and deferential ways pleasing her; whilst Captain Farmer had from the first filled her sensitive mind with a fear she could not overcome; a fear probably arising from the fact that though good-looking and well-shaped, his manner was often wild and abrupt. Moreover there was about him a general air of excitability that awed her, which though she was then unaware of the cause, was due to temporary fits of insanity from which he had suffered since birth.

A day came when Captain Murray asked her to become his wife and met with a refusal; she telling him, she was too young to think of marriage, and that though she liked, she did not love him. Seeing that he was repugnant to her, Captain Farmer had not proposed to her personally, but set about gaining her in what he considered a more certain way; this was to ask her father's permission to make her his wife. Beau Power was delighted at the prospect of ridding himself of the encumbrance of a daughter, especially when now on the verge of ruin he could satisfactorily dispose of her to an officer in the army, a man of old family, 'who offered the most liberal proposals which a large fortune enabled him to make.'

The bargain was closed without delay, and one evening Margaret was called into the shabby dining-room, the atmosphere of which was heavy with the smell of roast meat and whisky, where though long after dinner her father was still drinking his customary four glasses of punch. This from miserable experience, was known to be and dreaded as his worst hour. Pale and trembling, the child, yet in short frocks, stood at the foot of the table, her

wistful eyes striving to read the flushed and
frowning face of the tyrant, who roughly and
briefly told her that she was to marry Captain
Farmer. She heard in silence, scarce believing he was serious, but on learning that her
father meant what he said, she burst into
tears and refused to obey. Power who
allowed those he ruled to have no will but
his own, shouted out violent threats in his
semi-drunken fury, struck the table, stormed
and swore he would be obeyed, when she
escaped from the room and blindly sought
her own, situated at the top of the house,
a dingy little apartment sacred to her as a
sanctuary, the eaves of its sloping roof the
shelter-place of many nests, its high solitary
window looking down upon the river, the
worn bridge, and the island beyond with
its rushes. Here she gave vent to the grief
which shook, to the fear which overwhelmed
her, rebelling in the bitterness of her heart
against the fate which threatened her. The
dislike she had from the first felt towards
Captain Farmer, now deepened to repulsion :

23

the unknown was more terrible to this child than the miseries she could realise, though the latter were cruel enough: for as long as she could remember her home had been darkened by a man of violent temper and brutal manner, such as her future husband promised to be; and she remembered with self-pity the nervous apprehensions, the watchful terror, the strain of mind, the household had long endured. Was her future to be as her past?

One hope for her remained. Broken-spirited and ill-used as her mother was, she would surely rebel against her husband in his attempt to sacrifice his daughter. True, though affectionate in an impulsive and undiscerning way, she had from want of sympathy and insight, ever failed to understand her daughter's nature, and had never been drawn to her by that bond of union which is closer than relationship, which relationship itself frequently fails to establish. It might be however that having suffered in her own married life, she would in this point

recognise the misery that awaited her child
and strive to avert it: but Margaret was soon
to learn that her hopes in this direction were
ill-founded. For whilst the girl was still upon
her knees in tears, her mother entered the
room, and one glance at her face showed
that the sympathy and aid anxiously looked
for were missing. To Margaret's sob-choked
cry 'Oh mother have you heard?' the
answer came that she knew all and considered Margaret foolish to behave in such
a rebellious manner. She was a child with
romantic notions; books had filled her mind
with nonsense; her parents were the best
judges of how she should act. She should be
pleased and flattered to have a proposal from
Captain Farmer, instead of giving way to
foolish tears: for he was a young and a handsome man much in love with her; he was in a
good position and had fine prospects; what
more did she want?

As for not loving him, that was because she
had got absurd notions from reading poetry;
when girls grew up they had to think of other

things than love. What she should remember was that her father was a ruined man, who might be sold up and left without a home any day: that it was her duty to catch at this chance of a settlement which would be a relief to her family, and that as Captain Farmer's wife she would have an opportunity of advancing her sisters' and perhaps her brothers' prospects. At all events marry she must, and without delay.

There now seemed no chance of escape from a marriage which she feared and loathed: without a friend capable of aiding or protecting her, she was driven into that innermost loneliness where so much of her life from childhood upwards had been spent. Her white face with its imploring eyes only made her father more furious, and if possible more determined she should marry Farmer, to whom he was probably under obligations. The force of her grief was therefore reserved for night, when in the silence broken only by the surge of the river, and the swish of the rushes, she sobbed herself to sleep that brought her terrifying dreams.

The heartlessness of Power is emphasised
by the fact that before the marriage took
place he had been told by Farmer's relatives
that the latter had been insane, but this fact
carefully kept from Margaret did not alter
her father's plans. News of the intended
marriage becoming known, the relatives of the
family and neighbours regarded it as a violence
done to the girl and an act of tyranny on the part
of her father ; but the increased unpopularity
with which he was regarded only made him
more forcibly resent his daughter's tears. As
for the bridegroom elect, he was by no means
to be put from his purpose by the shrinking
repugnance and open fear shown him by the
child. And so day after day passed bringing
her nearer and more near to what she dreaded,
until cowed into submission, and by bitterness of suffering made temporarily indifferent
to her fate, she became a wife at the
age of fifteen years and six months: the
marriage being celebrated in the parish
church of Clonmel, 'according to the rites
and ceremonies of the United Church of

England and Ireland' on the 7th of March 1804.

The result of this union may readily be anticipated; for years afterwards its brutality and misery impressed her mind. Once in speaking of this time she told a friend she had not been long under her husband's roof when it became evident that he was subject to fits of insanity; that 'he frequently treated her with personal violence, that he used to strike her on the face, pinch her till her arms were black and blue, lock her up whenever he went abroad, and often left her without food till she felt almost famished.'

His insane jealousy, his capricious temper, and arrogant bearing, made life a long-continued terror during the three months which she lived with him. At the end of this time his regiment was ordered to the Curragh of Kildare, when summoning such spirit as was left her, she refused to accompany him. He therefore allowed her to remove to her father's house, there to remain for the present.

It happened that a few days after he had

reached the Curragh, Farmer had an argument with his colonel, on whom in a moment of frenzy he drew his sword. This act being mercifully set down to insanity, Farmer was spared a trial by court-martial and its consequences, and allowed to sell his commission. His friends then obtained for him an appointment in the East India Company's service.

Before starting for India he strove to persuade his wife to accompany him abroad, but having the memory of recent sufferings fresh in her mind, she refused, when he did her the service of taking himself out of her life for ever.

And in this way ended the prelude to a career whose strange surprises, emotional episodes, brilliant success and tragic ending, must possess a seductive charm for all students of life.

CHAPTER II

An Unprotected Wife—An Unhappy House—A
Hateful Position—Lord Blessington appeared
upon the Scene—A Tragedy in the Fleet—
Freedom and Marriage—An Irish Welcome
The Mansion in St James's Square.

THE return of Margaret Farmer to her father's
home was made unwelcome, and it seemed
as if her unhappiness was destined to continue:
for her parents resented as they might a reproof, the fact of her marriage having turned
out miserably; and instead of regarding her
as its victim, treated her as if she were
responsible for its wretchedness. Not only
had she been of no service in helping to marry
her sister Ellen, or in forwarding the fortunes
of her family, but she had come back upon
their hands a burden.

Her father behaved towards her with morose-

ness, her mother assumed the airs of a martyr,
and her only comfort was in her brothers and
sisters, who pitied her as openly as they
dared without drawing down on themselves
the fire and fury of the head of the house.
As the cool resentment with which she was
at first received gradually wore away, it was
succeeded by a more active hostility. She
was now referred to as an interloper, whose
experience was likely to interfere with her
sister's prospects of settlement.

Her sister Ellen, a year younger than
Margaret, had already gained much admiration in Clonmel society and at garrison
balls, and was regarded by her parents as
the beauty of the family. With classically-
cut features, a pale clear complexion, large
calm blue eyes, her face had the symmetry
and repose of statuary, her figure was excessively graceful, and like her sister she
possessed a natural air of refinement and
dignity. So far as regularity and modelling
of feature went, she had the advantage of
her elder sister : but the latter had an intelli-

gence and piquancy of expression that gave her a fascination which Ellen, cold and placid, entirely lacked. Her youngest sister Mary Anne was then a child of about eight.

Even at this time Beau Power, who every day advanced deeper into the mire of debt, managed to keep open house; and not only entertained the officers stationed in the garrison, but also the judges and lawyers who visited the town during the assizes. Like most men who are tyrants at home, he could be bland and amusing abroad; and he readily gathered round his table men willing to enjoy his hospitality.

Amongst such were not wanting many who ardently admired the wife of sixteen summers, beautiful, intelligent, and unhappy, whose situation, deprived as she was of the protection of a husband or the care of a father, seemed to make way for their advances. Wherever she went she was pursued by suitors who sought to take her from her father's house. Amongst them was a man of fascinating personality, wealthy, and connected with the nobility, whom she had learned to care for and with whom she would have gone had she not heard that he was married; when she refused to destroy another woman's happiness even to secure her own.

Another suitor was Captain Thomas Jenkins of the 11th Light Dragoons whose regiment was stationed in the neighbouring town of Tullow, a member of an old Hampshire family, with an income of between six and eight thousand a year, amiable and generous, who added polished manners to the attraction of a handsome person. For a long time she refused to listen to his proposals and would probably have continued to do so, had not news reached her that Farmer after spending a couple of years abroad during which he had taken to drink, had now left the East India Company's service, and was on his way home with the avowed intention of forcing her to live with him.

No more terrifying prospect could be placed before her. She had for nearly three years suffered in silence the wretchedness of her humiliating position in her father's home which every day became more hateful; but life with a drunkard and a lunatic to whom she knew her parents would willingly give her up, would be unendurable. In her plight she turned for advice to Major, afterwards Sir Edward Blakeney, then on duty with his regiment in Clonmel, an elderly, kind-hearted, honourable man in whose friendship she trusted. As the result of her consultation with him, she left her father's house with Captain Jenkins whom, without loving, she esteemed as a friend, when he took her to live in Hampshire.

The position which seemed forced upon her by circumstances was odious to her, and left behind it a memory which cloud-like came between her and the sun of her happiness throughout her life. Her most earnest efforts were, not only by her demeanour but by her dress, to avoid everything which might remind her or others of her situation; and in this she was seconded by Captain Jenkins.

No greater delicacy, respect, or affection could be shown her were she his wife; yet the costly presents which he delighted in lavishing on her and she found herself obliged to accept, humiliated her. In the meantime her position was perhaps rendered less trying by the conduct of his family: for seeing her retiring manners and the good influence she exercised over him in preventing the ruinous extravagance in which he had formerly indulged, they by kindness and friendship treated her in every way as if she were his wife.

She had been living under the protection of Captain Jenkins for some six years when Lord Blessington then a widower came on a visit to the latter for a few weeks hunting. The Earl was not unknown to Margaret Farmer; for soon after her marriage, the Tyrone Militia, whose Lieutenant-Colonel was Viscount Mountjoy afterwards Earl of Blessington, had been stationed at Clonmel; so that it was in Ireland she had first met the man whose life she was fated to influence, whose rank and wealth aided her beauty and talents to exercise the brilliant sway they were later to obtain.

This renewal of acquaintance soon led to warmer feelings on the Earl's part. His admiration of Margaret Farmer gradually deepened, until at last he offered to make her his wife, contingent on her obtaining a divorce from her husband: he meanwhile providing her with a home, but treating her merely as one to whom he was engaged. The prospect of being relieved from her present position which time had not helped to render less humiliating, and of becoming a wife, were hailed by her with infinite relief and gratitude. Her feelings underwent no change towards Captain Jenkins, whom without loving she had liked. He had now to be consulted; and on learning Lord Blessington's intentions, set aside all considerations of self which would interfere with her chances of happiness.

Lord Blessington therefore took a house in Manchester Square London, for Margaret

Farmer, who lived here in charge of her brother Robert, who was now made agent for the Blessington estates. And no sooner had she parted from Captain Jenkins, than Lord Blessington sent him a cheque for ten thousand pounds, the presumed value of the jewels and apparel given by Jenkins to Margaret Farmer, which he accepted. Before taking up her residence in Manchester Square it had been stipulated by her that she and the Earl should live apart until such time as her divorce could be obtained, a compact which was strictly kept; a statement made on the authority of Mr Taggart, a friend of Lord Blessington whom he represented ' in selecting this establishment.

Before the divorce was obtained, however death had freed her. On Farmer's return from India he had remained in London where he sought the society of those not calculated to cure his love of drink. In October 1817 he obtained an appointment in the service of the Spanish Patriots, and before quitting England betook himself one night to bid farewell to some boon companions whose habits had brought them to the King's Bench Prison. In those days prisoners of the Fleet were allowed to receive and to entertain their friends in what fashion they pleased so long as they paid, and Captain Farmer had been a frequent and a riotous visitor to certain individuals there confined.

On the occasion of this his last visit, the party had finished four quarts of rum and were all drunk when Farmer rose to leave. He had no sooner stated his intention of quitting them, than his companionship being coveted by his friends, they locked the door to prevent his departure. Now fearing they were going to keep him all night as they had done more than once before, he rushed to the window which he threw up, and threatened to jump out if they did not set him free. His threat was met with a chorus of drunken and incredulous laughter which set this valiant man upon his mettle, and to show them he was ready to keep his word he scrambled out upon the ledge where he remained arguing solemnly with the merry group inside, whose faces flushed by drink were lighted by wax candles standing on a liquor-stained table. Suddenly, by a heedless move he lost his balance, fell, and frantically clutched with nerveless fingers the ledge from which he hung some seconds, his wild eyes taking their last look on life in staring at the awed group within ; his sobered mind realising that certain death waited him in the darkness yawning below.

As his companions, helpless to save because of their muddled brains and paralysed limbs, still looked, they saw the space his head had filled, suddenly become empty, and whilst holding each his breath, heard a sickening thud. Then all was still. Farmer in whom when found, life still flickered, was carried to the Middlesex Hospital where he died next day.

There was now nothing to prevent the Earl's marriage with the woman he loved ; a marriage which four months later, on the 16th of February 1818 took place by special licence at the Bryanston Square Church, when Margaret Farmer became Marguerite Countess of Blessington; and in this manner was raised to a rank she was in all ways fitted to fill, and gained a title eventually to be associated with the most brilliant circle of her day, a title which yet conjures up a host of memorable associations.

Lady Blessington had not at this time reached her thirtieth year, and the joyousness of life lay before her. The attractions of her youth had deepened with her years; education, sorrow, and experience had united in giving her mind a breadth and training which her face expressed. The wistfulness of her eyes, the sweetness of her smile, the piquancy of her features, her grace of movement, her charm of manner, and the melody of her voice combined to make her a fascinating woman.

The man who loved her was but seven years her senior and like herself was Irish by birth and descent. His father Viscount Mountjoy and Baron Mountjoy in the County of Tyrone

had been a well-known figure in the Irish
parliament where he had warmly advocated
the claims of Catholics to equality of legisla-
tion ; and had taken an active part in the
suppression of the rebellion of 1798 when he
was shot in the battle of New Ross at the
head of his regiment. At the age of seventeen the second husband of Margaret Farmer
had been left lord of himself and of a handsome fortune which throughout his life he
endeavoured to spend right royally. He had
been educated at Eton and at Christ Church
Oxford, and at twenty-three had been appointed Lieutenant-Colonel of the Tyrone
Militia. In 1809 he was elected a repre-
sentative peer for Ireland, and two years
before his second marriage, had been advanced
to the Earldom of Blessington.

Loaded with wealth and honour the world
was a sunny place in his sight : young and
handsome he accepted the favours it offered
him and enjoyed its pleasures to the full.
No brighter youth danced in satin breeches
and velvet coat at Almacks; none gayer

gave delicious suppers in the lamp-lit bowers
of Vauxhall Gardens. Tall, vigorous, bright-
eyed and winsome, generous to extravagance
and sweet-natured, he was caressed by all
who like himself loved gaiety and seized the
sunshine of the passing hour.

Byron remembered him 'in all the glory
of gems and snuff-boxes, and uniforms and
theatricals, sitting to Strolling the painter to
be depicted as one of the heroes of Agincourt.'
For theatricals he had a special taste and
regarded himself as an accomplished actor.
Indeed for several years he entertained his
friends at Mountjoy Forest, Tyrone, for three
or four weeks at a time with plays performed
in a spacious theatre he had built, and acted
by players from Dublin and London, he taking prominent parts in the casts : his house
crowded with guests who were overwhelmed
with the most lavish hospitality. In London
also he concerned himself with the drama,
and was one of the noblemen who assisted at
the farewell banquet given to John Philip
Kemble in July 1817.

As Viscount Mountjoy, George the Fourth had shown him the favour of his countenance, and when the Viscount became an Earl, his Majesty who was busy in trumping up charges against his Queen, said 'I hope I shall find in Blessington as warm a friend as I found in Mountjoy' to which the new peer replied that he was afraid the prosecution of her Majesty would make the King unpopular, and that he never could be the advocate of a measure that might lead to recrimination.

When about twenty-seven years old, Lord Blessington had met a lady named Brown, whose beauty was the means of parting her from her husband, a major in the army. Enthusiastic in all things but especially in love, the gallant carried away the woman who charmed him, buying a residence for her at Worthing and another in Portman Square. She bore him two children, a boy and a girl, before her husband was considerate enough to die, when my lord made her my lady, in gratitude for which she bore him two other children also a girl and a boy, Lady Harriet Anne Frances Gardiner, and the Right Hon. Luke Wellington, Viscount Mountjoy.

Soon after the birth of this legitimate heir, the mother became ill, when her husband decided to take her to France with the hope of benefiting her health. They had not journeyed further than St Germains when she retired from life, and furnished my lord with an opportunity of indulging his theatrical tastes by providing a funeral which became the talk of three European capitals and cost him from three to four thousand pounds. This event took place in September 1814, and three years and five months later Lord Blessington married Margaret Farmer. In the beginning of his career the Earl's income was thirty thousand a year, but owing to his extravagant habits and the various encumbrances charged upon the estate, it had dwindled to between twenty-three and twenty-four thousand a year at the time of his second marriage ; a splendid fortune in itself for the daughter of a ruined squireen.

Soon after this marriage Lord Blessington took his bride to Ireland when they stayed at Mountjoy Forest. Preparations for their visit had been made; the tenantry who worshipped a landlord who never had evicted one of them nor allowed them to be distressed for rent, formed themselves into a lane miles long, to hail his arrival and that of his beautiful bride; their faces lit with welcome, their voices ringing blessings, their arms outstretched in friendship to my lady and my lord. And no sooner had the carriage passed than they followed, a wild, shouting, gesticulating throng, whose hearts bounding in the joy of greeting touched the hearts of those they cheered : a greeting whose accents sounded with old familiar sweetness to one of those who heard.

The residence which they were to occupy for a short time had been decorated and furnished anew, with what extravagance may be imagined when it is stated that Lady Blessington found her private sitting-room 'hung with crimson Genoa silk velvet, trimmed

with gold bullion fringe, and all the furniture
of equal richness—a richness that was only
suited to a state room in a palace.' Mountjoy
Forest now became the scene of the most
extravagant hospitality. Dinners, balls, parties
followed each other in rapid succession; every
day had its fresh form of entertainment, and
neither exertion nor wealth was spared to
mark the significance of the bridal visit. But
she whom it was intended to honour, seems
to have taken little enjoyment in this continual revel: the fact being that the country
soon bored her, though not so much as its
rough - hewn deep - drinking gentry, whose
hearts were honest but whose manners were
unpolished: who though in some cases the
descendants of native princes, were in most
instances illiterate.

She therefore induced her husband to leave
Ireland much sooner than he had intended,
and to return to London where she was anxious
to begin her career as a leader of society.
The house she had formerly occupied in
Manchester Square was given up and a

mansion rented in St James's Square that was fitted up with all the magnificence which taste could suggest or money purchase.

Lord Blessington's high position, varied tastes, and engaging manners had made him acquainted with the most distinguished personages in London; politicians, writers, statesmen, poets, and travellers. And they being made welcome to a palatial home where they found a hostess beautiful and accomplished, frankly desirous to please, willing to give homage to genius, not unwilling to receive praise, quick to perceive merit, with all the tact of the Celt, gentle-voiced and charming, readily came again and again bringing others in their train; until by degrees the mansion in St James's Square became noted as a centre where the most brilliant and distinguished men of the day congregated around one of the most fascinating women of the period.

In her spacious drawing-rooms with their frescoed ceilings, their chandeliers of crystal and silver, their priceless pictures, and oriental embroideries, and their general air of splendour,

Whigs for awhile forgot their hatred of Tories, men of fashion rubbed shoulders with men of letters, and royal dukes were as humble subjects before her whom nature had made regal. Here came my Lord Palmerston to divest himself of the cares of state and hear John Philip Kemble, now retired, speak of his past glories : here Tom Moore related to his hostess the last news received from Byron, her meeting with whom was later on to form an episode in her life : here young Lord Castlereagh, handsome, extravagant, talented, a poet and a traveller, gained more attention than his gifts alone would have obtained for him, from the fact that he had figured in a romance with a voluptuous Venetian whose husband had shot him through the arm. Sir Thomas Laurence came to see her whose beauty had given him the opportunity of painting his finest portrait : and with him his brother in art Wilkie, Samuel Rogers, banker and poet, Earl Russell, James Scarlett afterwards Lord Abinger, Lord Brougham, vehement and witty, Jekyll, and Erskine, and Earl Grey my lady's warm admirer and devoted friend, besides a host of others, congregated in her home.

Amongst literary men bidden to her house were Byron's friend the Hon. Douglas Kinnaird, who had adapted Fletcher's comedy 'The Merchant of Bruges' which was produced at Drury Lane; William Jerdan, John Galt, and Dr Samuel Parr.

William Jerdan was then an author of repute having published a number of novels and was moreover editor of *The Literary Gazette*, a journal whose praise or blame made or marred a book, so great was its influence in literary circles. Witty and wise by turns, he was always warmly welcomed by his hostess and became her frequent guest. 'The more I saw and knew of her' he wrote years later 'the more I loved her kind and generous nature, her disposition to be good to all, her faithful energy to serve her friends. Full of fine taste, intelligence, and imagination, she was indeed a lovable woman; and by a wide circle she was regarded as the centre of a highly intellectual and brilliant society.'

John Galt a native of Ayrshire who has been described as being as wise as a sage and as simple as a child, equally shrewd and credulous, as eminently practical as he was fancifully imaginative, was likewise her devoted friend. He had begun his career in commerce but launching into poetry had produced tragedies which were pronounced by Sir Walter Scott 'the worst ever seen.' He had travelled and had become acquainted with Lord Byron of whom he delighted to talk; and his powers of persuasion may be estimated when it is stated that he induced Colburn to issue a monthly publication called *The Rejected Theatre* that contained plays refused by London managers, whose want of judgment and enterprise were in this manner cruelly exposed and they brought to shame. His own plays of course held a great part of this magazine, which it is fair to state survived a year. What perhaps gained him a place in Lady Blessington's drawing-room, was the fact that he had soon after her marriage made a genuine success by publishing his novel *The Ayrshire Legatees,* which first ran through *Blackwood's Magazine*, and so exalted him that he boasted that his literary resources were superior to Sir Walter Scott, with whom he resolved to compete in historical fiction.

A more remarkable figure was Dr Samuel Parr who appeared at her receptions in a full dress-suit of black velvet, a powdered wig covering his massive head, his rugged features lighted by piercing eyes which he boasted he could 'inflict' on those he wished to subdue. Dr Parr who was at this time drawing near his eightieth year was a learned scholar, a prebend of St Paul's, a rector, an author, an ex-schoolmaster, and a contributor to the *British Critic*.

When a schoolmaster at Stanmore it had been his custom to stalk through the town in a dirty striped morning-gown; to flog his pupils with vigour; and to arrange that their fights should take place at a spot where he could see and enjoy them from his study windows.

In 1820 he caused a sensation by entering a

solemn protest in the parish prayer-book against the omission from the liturgy of George the Fourth's injured wife Queen Caroline. Moreover he visited her Majesty and was appointed her first chaplain. The doctor was an ardent lover of tobacco and smoked his twenty pipes regularly of an evening; nay, during intervals of the services he conducted, he used to retire to the vestry that he might enjoy a whiff: but on being introduced to Lady Blessington he vowed he would sacrifice his pipe to spend an evening in her company, and no higher estimate of the pleasure she afforded him could he give. So delighted was he with her graciousness, and so impressed by her appearance, that from the period of his first visit he styled her 'the most gorgeous Lady Blessington' a phrase that passed into common use amongst her friends.

One evening some three years after her establishment at St James's Square, the groom of the chambers announced a name that was unfamiliar, and there entered her drawing-room, brilliant with the light of innumerable

candles and voiceful with the sound of a
hundred tongues, a young Frenchman then
strange to her, whose history was subsequently to become intimately interwoven
with her own; whose friendship, keeping
loyal, sweetened her life and survived her
death. He had been brought to her reception by his brother-in-law the Comte de
Grammont both of them being on a brief
visit to London. This was Count Alfred
D'Orsay then just one - and - twenty, a descendant on the maternal side from the Kings
of Wurtemberg, and on the paternal side
from one of the most ancient families in
France. His singularly handsome appearance
was a hereditary gift, his father known in his
youth as Le Beau D'Orsay, having elicited
from Napoleon the remark that he would make
an admirable model for Jupiter. The beauty
of Count Alfred D'Orsay's person was enhanced by his great physical strength; moreover he was brilliant as a conversationalist,
soldierly in bearing, a lover of art, skilled in
all manly exercises and elegant in his attire;

one in fact whom nature richly endowed, and whom fate deigned to figure in romance.

At an early age he had entered the *Garde de Corps* of the restored Bourbon ; he had already shown great skill in painting ; his modelling was later to bring him fame as a sculptor; whilst his journal kept in London was, when shown to Lord Byron, pronounced by the poet 'a very extraordinary production and of a most melancholy truth in all that regards high life in England.'

With the courtly manners of the old *régime*, with an ardent admiration for women's beauty, an appreciation for talent, endowed with a sunny youth regarding whose undefinable future it was interesting to speculate, he stood before Lady Blessington a dazzling personality in a crowd where all were brilliant. For a moment, as it were, the circles of their lives touched to part for the present; for D'Orsay was soon obliged to return to France ; and at this time she had no intention of taking that journey which was destined to become so eventful in her career.

With the change in her fortunes Lady
Blessington was not forgetful of her family.
Indeed a rich generosity was a distinguish-
ing trait amongst her many fine qualities.
Long-expected ruin having overtaken her
worthless father, he with his wife left Clonmel
and settled in Dublin; and they having no
means of subsistence were supported for the
remainder of their lives by Lady Blessington
and her sister Ellen. The latter had been
invited to England by Margaret before her
marriage with the Earl, and had become the
wife of John Home Purves, son of a Scotch
baronet. After the death of her first husband
with whom she did not live happily, she
married in 1828, the Right Honourable Charles
Manners Sutton, son of the Archbishop of
Canterbury, and for eighteen years Speaker
of the House of Commons on retiring
from which office he received a pension of
four thousand a year and was raised to the
peerage as Viscount Canterbury.

Her second and youngest sister Mary Anne
styled Marianne by the Countess, was adopted

and educated by her, and eventually married to an old French noble the Comte St Marsault, from whom she soon separated. Her eldest brother Michael had got a commission, probably through Lady Blessington's interest, in the 2nd West India Regiment and died abroad; whilst her second and youngest brother Robert was, as already mentioned, agent of the Blessington estates.

Four years after her marriage, at the close of the summer 1822, she and her husband resolved to leave town for the coming winter; but their choice of residences lay far apart, he wishing to stay in Ireland whilst she desired to visit Italy. Whether her reluctance to live in her native land was due to the unpleasantness of early associations, or to some slight received from the Earl's sisters, one of whom was wife of the Bishop of Ossery, cannot be said; but the fact remains she never visited Ireland a second time as Countess of Blessington. Regarding the unwillingness she had expressed to take up her residence at Mountjoy Forest, John Galt writes to her at some length, in a letter dated July 27, 1822 which says :—

'MY DEAR MADAM,—On Monday evening I was so distinctly impressed with the repugnance which your ladyship feels at the idea of going to Ireland, that I entered entirely into your feelings ; but upon reflection, I cannot recall *all* the reasonableness of the argument— a circumstance so unusual with respect to your ladyship's reasons in general, that I am led to think that some other cause at the moment must have tended to molest you, and to lend the energy of its effect to the expressions of your reluctance. For I have often remarked that the gnat's bite, or a momentary accident, will sometimes change the whole complexion of the mind for a time. But even though nothing of the sort had happened, the scores and hundreds, amounting to thousands of the poor Irish in quest of employment whom I have met on the road and seen landing here, and the jealousy with which they are viewed by the common people, and the parochial burdens which they may occasion in the contemplation of the best of the community, many of whom are loud in their reflections on the Irish absentees, all combine to form such a strong case for my lord's journey, that nothing but the apprehension of your ladyship's indisposition can be pled against it. The journey, however, to be really useful, should be one of observation only, and I am sure you will easily persuade him to make it so, and to be resolved not to listen to any complaint with a view to decision in Ireland, or to embark in any new undertaking. If he once allow himself to be appealed to on the spot, he must of necessity become affected by local circumstances and individual impartialities by which, instead of doing *general* good (all a personage of his rank can do), he will become the mere administrator of petty relief, which in their effect may prove detrimental to higher objects; and were he to engage in new undertakings—to say nothing of pecuniary considerations—his thoughts would become occupied with projects which, of every kind of favouritism, is the most fatal to the

utility of a public character, such as my
lord seems now fairly set in to become. In
speaking thus, I address you more as an
intellect than a *lady*, and the interest I take
in all that concerns my friends must be
accepted as the only excuse I can offer for
the freedom.

' I really know not what apology to make
to your ladyship for all this impertinence; but
somehow, since I have had the honour and
pleasure of knowing you and my lord so
freely, I feel as if we were old friends; indeed,
how can it be otherwise, for no other human
beings, unconnected by the common ties,
have ever taken half so much interest in
at once adding to my enjoyments and consideration. I am sensible not only of having
acquired a vast accession of what the world
calls advantages, but also friends who seem
to understand me, and that too at a period
when I regarded myself as in some degree
quite alone, for all my early intimates were
dead. Your ladyship must therefore submit
to endure a great deal more than perhaps I

ought to say on so short an acquaintance;
but as minds never grow old, and frankness
makes up at once the intimacy of years, I find
myself warranted to say that I am almost an
ancient, as I am ever your ladyship's faithful
and sincere friend.'

It is almost needless to say that Lady
Blessington's wishes were carried out by a
husband so devoted to her; and in the month
of August 1822 they made preparations
to leave England for an indefinite period. A
journey abroad was in those days considered
a formidable undertaking especially for people
of rank and fashion, who took with them their
own carriages and servants, kitchen utensils
and table appointments, not to speak of huge
boxes containing their wardrobes. Before quitting the home where she had known such
splendour, Lady Blessington tells us, that she
went through the rooms looking at the pictures
and the furniture with a melancholy feeling
she did not expect to experience in starting
on a tour to which she had long looked
forward. Almost at the moment of her

departure she wished she were not going. 'What changes, what dangers may come before I sleep again beneath this roof. Perhaps I may never—but I must not give way to such sad forebodings' she writes in the diary she now began to keep: and she adds a passage regarding the pain she felt at taking leave of friends; for 'even those whose society afforded little pleasure, assume a new interest at parting.'

Leaving London on the 25th they reached Calais two days later, having made the journey in an overcrowded packet under gloomy and threatening skies that lent a leaden-green colour to the sea. They reached Paris by the end of the month; and the following day, September the 1st was her birthday, whose recurrence, she writes, is enough to produce melancholy recollections. 'In England I should experience these doleful feelings, but at Paris *tristesse* and sentimentality would be misplaced; so I must look *couleur de rose*, and receive the congratulations of my friends on adding another year to my age; a subject far from meriting congratulations when one has passed thirty. Youth is like health, we never value the possession of either until they have begun to decline.'

Whilst in Paris they met Tommy Moore whom they asked to dinner. My lady thought the dinners at the hotel execrable, but she detested going to a restaurant as was even then the fashion for English people : consequently she preferred a bad dinner at home, and this the poet was invited to share, though she thought it unworthy of his acceptance. 'A mouth that utters such brilliant things' she writes 'should only be fed on dainty ones ; and as his skill in gastronomy nearly equals his skill in poetry, a failure in one art must be almost as trying to his temper, as the necessity of reading a failure in the other ; nay it would be worse, for one may laugh at a bad poem, but who has philosophy enough to laugh at a bad dinner?' She goes on to say that a perfect French dinner is like the conversation of a highly-educated man ; enough of the raciness of the inherent natural quality remains to gratify his taste, but rendered more attractive by the manner in which it is presented.

'An old nobleman used to say that he could judge of a man's birth by the dishes he preferred, but above all by the vegetables : truffles, morels, mushrooms, and peas in their infancy, he designated as aristocratic vegetables ; but all the vast stock of beans, full-grown peas, carrots, turnips, parsnips, cauliflowers, onions etc. he said were only fit for the vulgar.'

Moore spent some time with them and took the Countess to La Montagne Russe, 'a very childish but exhilarating amusement' in which the poet frequently indulged. She thought it 'pleasant to observe with what a true zest he enters into every scheme of amusement, though the buoyancy of his spirits and resources of his mind render him so independent of such means of passing time. His is a happy temperament that conveys the idea of having never outlived the sunshine.'

The time she passed in a Parisian hotel does not seem to have been pleasant, for the indifference of foreign ears to noise was as remarkable then as now. The neighing of horses and the rumble of wheels in the courtyard, the swearing of coachmen and the grumbling of porters, the shrill voices of women, the singing of lacqueys, the talking of a parrot, the barking of a dog, and the ringing of bells prevented her from sleeping. Then her own servants began to murmur at what they considered their hardships and to sigh for the fleshpots of England. The maids longed for their tea and toast ; the men felt the loss of their beef and beer. 'I have observed' she says 'that persons accustomed from infancy to the utmost luxury, can better submit to the privations occasioned by travelling, than can their servants.'

She was not sorry to leave Paris after a stay of ten days, and one morning the court-yard was full of their carriages which were being packed anew. A crowd of valets and footmen were hoisting heavy trunks into their places; the maids had their arms full of cushions and books for my lady's special carriage ; the courier went to and fro examining the springs ; the major domo saw that the plate was safely stored away in the chaise seat. In the 'capacious fourgon' was already packed various articles considered indispensable to the traveller, such as a patent brass bed, easy chairs and sofas, readily folded, *batteries de cuisine* for the benefit of the cook who accompanied them, and cases that held 'delicate *chapeaux, toques, bérets* and bonnets too fragile to bear the less easy motion of leathern band-boxes crowning imperials.' No wonder that Lady Blessington waiting in her room above, heard a Frenchman express his wonder at the strangeness of these foreigners and ask if all these coaches and this luggage belonged to the one proprietor. When answered in the affirmative he remarked 'One would suppose that instead of a single family a regiment at least was about to move. How many things those people require to satisfy them.'

On leaving London Lady Blessington had taken with her Mary Anne Power her youngest sister; and having met Count de D'Orsay in Paris, they invited him to join them, which he willingly did, but not until they had reached Avignon. A pleasure-seeking party they travelled with leisurely dignity through Switzerland and the South of France, engaging in some places a whole hotel at an exorbitant price, seeing all that was curious or interesting, and scattering money with a liberality supposed to belong to royalty. At Avignon they were visited by the poet laureate of the town who presented them with a congratulatory ode and retired from their presence happy in the possession of a donation, leaving them wondering if as he stated, he lived on his wits, how he could exist on so slender a capital : at Nice they were greeted by school children dressed in their holiday attire, who offered them bouquets; at Aix they received on leaving, farewell gifts of orange-flower water, bonbons, and roses ; so that their tour was a triumphant progress such as would be impossible in these later, more prosaic days of undignified haste.

The diary kept by Lady Blessington during her travels is mainly devoted to descriptions of, and comments on places visited and sights that impressed. All that would have abounded with interest for the modern reader—vignettes of domestic life, etchings of herself and her companions, touches of nature which lend human interest to everyday occurrences—are omitted from volumes intented for the public. The pages which are most interesting being those in which she describes her meeting for the first time with Lord Byron; this taking place in Genoa, a city she reached after nearly eight months of travel.

CHAPTER III

Lord Byron—·A Hero of Romance and an Object of
Hatred—Storm in the Social Atmosphere—In
Venice—The Rosiest Romance of His Life—A
Bride of Sixteen—Inexorable Fate—In Ravenna
—A Poet's Love-Letter—A Philosophic Husband
—Count Guiccioli becomes Uncivil—Strife and
Separation—Byron is summoned—A Common
Disturber—In Pisa—A Ghost-Haunted Palace—
Banishment—A New Residence sought—The
Villa at Albero—Lady Blessington's Hopes—
Lines written in Her Diary.

AT this time Lord Byron, as a poet and as
a man, exercised a fascination difficult for
later generations to appreciate; a fascination
due to the brilliancy of his genius, to the
beauty of his person, to - the mystery and
melancholy with which he endeavoured to
enwrap himself, and to the reputation
gained for the extravagance and romance of
his amours.

The descendant of 'those Byrons of

Normandy who had accompanied William the Conqueror into England,' he had the hot blood of adventurous ancestors in his veins: and whilst yet a youth had plunged into the lower depths of life from which he had returned saturated with a cynicism he never failed to express. Before reaching his majority he had delighted the town with his *Hours of Idleness* and punished his critics in *English Bards and Scotch Reviewers;* after which, chiefly from a desire to escape from the solitude that even at so early a period closed around his inner life,—that solitude from which even in the midst of crowds the poet is sure to suffer—and partly to dissipate the restlessness which is the travailing of genius, he had travelled through Italy and Spain to Turkey and Greece at a time when such a voyage was an uncommon occurrence.

On his return he had entered society for the first time. A peer of the realm, a poet, satirist, and traveller, dowered with the freshness and the grace of youth, daring in his aspirations, defiant of convention, hating the cant that encrusted his country, he stood before men a singular and unsolved problem, a genius not understood of his kind; one whose personality compelled admiration, indulgence in which, women intuitively recognised, might lead to danger.

The years that followed his return to England saw the publication of poems that with their metrical sweep, their seething passion, the melancholy sea-surge and fret of their moods, their bitter sarcasm, and open cynicism made his name known to the world. Then came the fatal mistake of his life, his marriage with Miss Milbanke, a paragon of perfection, wholly unfitted for and unworthy of the human nature of which poets are made. This event took place on the 2nd of January 1815, a day which to his impressionable mind was burdened by melancholy and darkened by presentiments which twelve months later were verified when his wife parted from him for ever. In December she had given birth to a daughter, and the following month started from London to visit her father in Leicestershire, taking leave of Byron with the utmost kindness, and on the understanding that he was shortly to join her. On her way she wrote him a letter full of affectionate playfulness: but soon after she had reached her destination, her father wrote to say she had resolved never to return to her husband.

This came upon Byron as a shock which the embarrassments of his fortunes at this time did not help him to bear. Eventually all efforts of his at reconciliation being rejected, he signed a deed of separation which left him 'without rational hope for the future.' This was but the beginning of a period of bitterness which was to last through his life. A storm in the social atmosphere now broke above his head, such as perhaps never assailed unhappy mortal before. Vague hints, dark insinuations, charges of profligacy and madness, swelled an overpowering chorus of accusation. Those envious of merit, those who wanting in virtue hasten to assail its violation in others that suspicion may be diverted from themselves; the entertaining society scandalmonger, the caricaturist, the vicious paragraphist, attacked with a strength of numbers and unity of force there was no counting or combating.

To invite him to her house was an act of civility for which few hostesses found sufficient courage : to defend him was to involve the defender in a suspicion of vileness. The charges of cant against his countrymen, his laughter at mediocrity, the scoffings at convention in which he had so frequently indulged, were now avenged : the gnats stung him to desperation; and three months after his wife had left him, he quitted England, never more to return.

Whilst in Switzerland, by the advice of his friend Madame de Stael, he made another effort at reconciliation, which like the first was rejected by Lady Byron. Then making a tour of the Bernese Alps he entered Italy, a country which, because of the colour of its skies and its seas, the light steeping its lands, the pagan-heartedness of its people, beautiful in themselves and worshippers of beauty in nature, had already thrown its fascination upon him.

He took up his residence in Venice and it was whilst living in this city of the sea, in fair spring weather, that the rosiest romance in his life was begun ; a romance which the limit of his days was not destined to outrun : for here it was in April 1819 that he met the young Countess Guiccioli, the descendant of an ancient and historic line, and the third wife of a wealthy old noble, to whom at the age of sixteen her parents had sacrificed her.

Looking back upon their meeting with the eyes of lovers, it seemed to the poet and the Countess, like an arrangement of inexorable fate. Madame Guiccioli had been bidden to a party by the Countess Benzoni, but on the evening it took place felt so fatigued that she wished to absent herself, and it was only in obedience to her veteran husband, proud of his fair child-wife, that she reluctantly con-sented to be present : whilst Byron who shrank from appearing in crowds, presented himself in this out of mere courtesy to the hostess whose friendship he valued. When requested by her to allow himself to be introduced to the Countess Guiccioli he at first declined, and later consented that he might not seem uncivil. In this way, irrespective of their own wills, ignorant of what it would entail, was their meeting brought about.

From the first each read in the eyes of the other the love which was mutually inspired; the love which later, in the silent water ways of this dream-like city, beneath the shadows of its grey arcades, in the languorous moonlight upon balconies, in the spacious *salons* of stately palaces, developed with frequent meeting: the secret they stored in their hearts, the more sacred for concealment; until at last the consciousness and assurance of their absorbing passion set their lives to music which their pulses marked, and made the world around a joy; they most joyous of all beneath the glamour and the glory of Italian skies.

But alas for their love this day-dream was not of long continuance, for before a month ended, a month which to them was but a

breath in the mouth of time, the Count
Guiccioli decided to leave Venice and return
to his home in Ravenna. The idea of parting
from the man but yesterday a stranger and
now the dearest of all upon earth; he who by
some strange power revealed her to herself
and woke such feelings as she had never known
her nature to possess, filled her with despair;
sickened her body till it weakened, and made
her think night had untimely darkened the
dawn of her day. The journey however was
begun, she seated pale and frail a wife of
sixteen summers beside her aged spouse in
his great coach covered with armorial bear-
ings and drawn by six horses, and during
the first day's journey she was thrice seized
by fainting fits.

She found strength however to write to
the poet wherever she rested on her route;
letters full of the fervent love that was burn-
ing up her life. In one of these she tells
him that the solitude of the place which before
had seemed intolerable, was now welcome to
her, for it gave her more opportunity to

dwell on the one object which occupied her heart. And then she promises to obey his wishes in avoiding all society, and to devote herself to reading and music, so that she might please him in every way, and prove worthy of him so far as she could : for her hope lay in their meeting once more, a hope without which life would be unbearable.

The day after writing this letter, whilst making the final stage of her journey, she was attacked by an illness for which there was no name, and carried to her home half dead. The sensitive nature of this child of the south gave way under the turbulence of her love; and the longing which tortured her mind brought a fever which consumed her body ; relief only coming when his letters reached her expressing his devotion and his determination to see her.

Towards the end of May she told him she had prepared all her friends for his visit which he might now make, and accordingly on the second of June he set out from La Mira where he had taken a summer villa, for Ravenna.

Scarcely had he entered the town when rumours that an English lord had arrived, spread abroad, on which Count Guiccioli suspecting the visitor's personality, hastened to his hotel to wait upon Byron whom he requested to call upon the Countess.

Bryon willingly obeyed and was taken to her residence, a great gloomy palace whose decay but added to its grandeur, whose solemn and melancholy atmosphere seemed to hold heavy records of crime and mystery. Mounting a magnificent staircase of white marble he was led to the woman he loved who lay in bed, from which her anxious relatives believed she would never rise. His pain and grief were intense, but only his eyes could tell her what he felt: for she was jealously guarded by the members of her family who were natives of Ravenna. His pen however could record something of his feelings, and in writing to his friend Murray he says of her: 'I do not know what I should do if she died, but I ought to blow my brains out—and I hope that I should,' whilst to

77

Hoppner he expresses his fears that she is going into a consumption. 'Thus it is with everything and everybody for whom I feel anything like a real attachment' he writes. '"War, death or discord doth lay siege to them." I never could keep alive a dog that I liked or that liked me.'

His presence beside her, the affection he showed her, did more to restore one who, like all sensitive and impressionable people, depended on the happiness of her mind for the health of her body, and in a couple of months she was pronounced convalescent.

Byron meanwhile remained in Ravenna.

This ancient town, an early home of Christian art, where Dante laid him down to rest, basks in the wide-stretching plain of Lombardy with its dense pine forest dividing the city from the sea, its giant poplars skirting dusty roads, its groves of olives with their grey-green leaves. Its sun-baked palaces have each their history, darker perhaps than their walls; its innumerable gardens feast the eyesight with their gorgeous colour: its

domed cathedral speaks of God invisible and
omnipotent; its gates are ancient, grey, and
grass grown; and its atmosphere is rich in
dreamy peace. What better or more fitting
place for love to flourish?

With these it grew apace until the Count
in his wisdom once more saw fit to visit his
estates and take his young wife with him;
when Byron, impatient and wilful, proposed
that she should fly with him. Such a proposi-
tion seemed astonishing to the mind of an
Italian wife; it was not that she would not
sacrifice everything for his love, but she considered an elopement unnecessary. Accordingly when she and her husband went to
Bologna, Byron by arrangement followed next
day. 'I cannot tell how our romance will
end' he writes 'but it hath gone on hitherto
most erotically. Such perils and escapes.
Juan's are as child's play in comparison.'

Having joined his friends at Bologna they
went to the theatre to see a representation of
Alfieri's Mirra; when a scene took place in
their box: for Byron then in an excitable con-

dition was so much affected by the play, that he was thrown into convulsions which produced 'the agony of reluctant tears' and choking shudders, witnessing which the sympathetic Countess became similarly affected. Next day both were 'ill, languid, and pathetic' as he narrates: nor did he soon recover.

Having spent near a month with them here, the Count went on to his Romagnese estates taking his wife with him but leaving her friend behind. This parting though it was for a brief time, filled Byron with melancholy, and his greatest pleasure in his loneliness was to visit her empty house at the hour when formerly he had sought her there; to cause her apartments to be opened and sit in them reading her books and writing in their pages. Then he would pass into the quaint, deserted garden, where he walked 'under a purple canopy of grapes' or sat by its fountain whose ripple alone disturbed the profound stillness of the place. Resting here one summer day he was so overcome by the pain of her absence, by the weirdness of his fancies, by nervous fears, and desolate forebodings that he burst into a passion of tears that wrung his soul.

Here too in this Italian garden with its wilderness of roses and the wealth of its perfumes, he wrote one of the most touching love letters in the language, on the last page of a copy of *Corinne*, belonging to the Countess.

'MY DEAREST TERESA,—I have read this book in your garden—my love, you were absent, or else I could not have read it. It is a favourite book of yours, and the writer was a friend of mine. You will not understand these English words, and *others* will not understand them—which is the reason I have not scrawled them in Italian. But you will recognise the handwriting of him who passionately loved you, and you will divine that, over a book which was yours, he could only think of love. In that word beautiful in all languages but most so in yours—*amor mio*—is comprised my existence here and hereafter. I feel I exist here and I fear that I shall exist hereafter—to *what* purpose you will decide: my destiny rests with you, and you are a woman seventeen years of age, and two out of a convent. I wish you had stayed there with all my heart—or at least that I had never met you in your married state.

'But this is too late. I love you and you love me, at least you say so and act as if you did so, which last is a great consolation in all events. But I more than love you and cannot cease to love you. Think of me sometimes when the Alps and the ocean divide us—but they never will unless you wish it.'

A few weeks after this was written Count Guiccioli and his wife returned to Bologna, but they had not been there long when the former found himself called to Ravenna on business and the latter discovered that illness prevented her from accompanying him. He therefore left her with Byron whose happiness now seemed as great as was his misery before. And the time of their joyousness was destined to be prolonged; for she soon concluded that the air of Ravenna was unsuited to her health,

which would soonest return to her in Venice :
to which effect she wrote to her husband.

That philosophic man agreed that she
should once more visit the City of the Sea
and that Lord Byron should be the companion of her voyage; and therefore they set
out for the place, precious to them as the
scene where first they had met, made beautiful by memories, a charmed place where they
were free to live the dreams they once had
dreamt there. In Venice they spent the
remaining months of summer, and early in
autumn they removed to the poet's villa at
La Mira.

In November the Count came to Venice
and presented his spouse with a paper of con-
ditions, regulations of hours and conduct and
morals, which he insisted on her accepting
and she persisted in refusing. 'I am' Byron
writes 'expressly it should seem excluded
by this treaty, as an indispensable preliminary : so that they are in high discussion, and
what the result may be I know not, particularly as they are consulting friends.' In case

that she finally parted with her husband, Byron had resolved to retire with her to France or to America, where under a changed name he would lead a quiet, provincial life.

After a considerable struggle, from which Byron held apart, the Countess reluctantly consented to return to Ravenna with her husband, and to hold no further communication with her lover. She therefore quitted Venice where Byron remained melancholy, ailing, and unable to make up his mind to visit England. The promise forced from the Countess that she would not write to the poet was soon broken, and ardent letters passed between them.

In one of these he declares that his state is most dreadful, he not knowing which way to decide—fearing on the one hand to compromise her by returning to Ravenna, and on the other dreading to lose all happiness by seeing her no more. 'I pray you, I implore you' he adds 'to be comforted, and to believe that I cannot cease to love you but with my life. It is not enough that I must leave you, it is not enough that I must fly from Italy with a heart deeply wounded, after having passed all my days in solitude since your departure, sick both in body and mind, but I must also have to endure your re-proaches without answering and without de-serving them. Farewell; in that one word is comprised the death of my happiness.'

He now decided on returning to England and the day of his departure was fixed. When the morning came on which he was to leave Venice, his packed boxes were taken to the gondola at his palace gate, he himself was dressed for the journey, and he merely waited for his firearms to be made ready. Suddenly acting on a presentiment, he declared that if all were not in order before the clock struck, he would not start that day. The last touches which were to mark his departure had not been given when the clock struck one; his gondola was unloaded and he never more saw the country for which he had been about to set out.

For next day brought him a letter from

Count Gamba, father of the Countess, stating that she was alarmingly ill, and fearful of the consequences of opposition, her family including her husband, entreated Byron to hasten to her: the letter furthermore promised there should be no more scenes between husband and wife such as had lately disturbed his lordship's domestic peace in Venice. Immediately he answered telling the Countess he soon would be beside her and that whether he ever left her again, would depend upon herself.

Arriving at Ravenna he took up his residence at a hotel, but only for a brief time until the quarters which he was permitted by the Count to rent at the Palazzo Guiccioli were made ready. Again the Countess enlivened by his presence rapidly recovered, and she was seen in his company everywhere. ·'Nobody seemed surprised; all the women on the contrary were, as it were, delighted with the excellent example.' The Count however after some six months had elapsed, professed to become uneasy: rumours of separation were in the air;

cardinals and priests were implicated; public opinion was dead against him for causing such a disturbance; all her relations were furious at his want of civility, and her father challenged him 'a superfluous valour for he don't fight, though suspected of two assassinations.' Finally Byron was warned not to take long rides in the pine forest without being on his guard.

Eventually on a petition of the much-suffering Countess and her family, a decree of separation came from Rome on condition that the wife should henceforth live beneath her father's roof. This her husband had opposed because of the allowance of two hundred a year—a miserable sum for a man of his wealth—which the same decree directed should be made her: and at the last moment he would have forgiven all, if she had consented never again to see Byron. This she declined to promise, and on the 16th of July 1820, she betook herself to her father's home, situated some fifteen miles from Ravenna, where occasionally she was visited by the poet.

Now in this year Count Gamba and his son engaged themselves in a movement for the freedom of Italy, and induced their friend Byron to join them in such enterprise. But in a little while suspicion falling on them, the Government ordered the Count to quit Ravenna within twenty-four hours, whilst the son was arrested at night and conveyed to the frontier. The Countess was now in despair, her nervous fears suggesting that if she left Ravenna she would see her lover no more ; and her fright was heightened when news was brought her secretly that her husband was appealing to Rome either to have her sent back to him, or to have her placed in a convent.

The exile of the Gambas was chiefly decreed in the hope that Byron would share their banishment; for knowing the freedom of his opinions, dreading his influence, jealous of his popularity, and exaggerating the extent of his means, which they feared might be used to spread liberalism, the Government had long desired his absence from Ravenna but had not dared to force the departure of an English subject. He was however unwilling to be driven from a city he liked so well; and whilst the Countess, her father, and her brother took refuge in Florence, he remained in Ravenna striving to get the decree of banishment against his friends rescinded.

Seeing the uselessness of his efforts he resolved to join them. On catching news of his departure the poor of Ravenna to whom he devoted a fourth part of his annual income, gathering together, presented a petition to the cardinal asking him to request Byron to remain. The place of the future residence of the Gamba family was for some time undecided; the Countess and her brother selecting Switzerland where they would be beyond the control of the Roman Government, Byron suggesting Tuscany, for he never could bear the Swiss 'and still less their English visitors.' Accordingly in August 1821 Count Gamba took a spacious palace known as the Casa Lanfranchi in Pisa. Here Byron joined them and at first was impressed by his new home, a noble marble pile 'which seemed built for eternity.' Its hall was enormous, its grand staircase had been designed by Michael Angelo, its windows looked down upon the slow sweeping Arno. But soon Byron's delight was disturbed ; and he writes to Murray that it had dungeons below, cells in the walls, and was full of ghosts, by whom the last occupants had been sorely bothered. Then he discovered a place where people had evidently been walled up ; all the ears in the palace had been regaled by all kinds of supernatural noises, and his valet begged leave to change his room and then refused to occupy his new apartment because there were more ghosts there than in the other.

Soon more material troubles beset him. Whilst riding out with a party of English and Scotch, they had a brawl with a soldier who had insulted one of the party, some of whom were arrested. The offending soldier was shortly afterwards stabbed whilst riding through the streets by one of his own countrymen, presumably a partisan of Byron's, and though the wounded man recovered, his friends threatened vengeance with the dagger. The affray caused a sensation, all kinds of investigations were made, finally the Tuscan Government thought itself called upon to interfere, and Count Gamba and his son received notice to quit Tuscany within four days.

As the Countess was obliged to live beneath her father's roof, Byron's removal was a foregone conclusion.

Again the scene of their future home was discussed, and South America was spoken of as a fitting place, but eventually Genoa was decided upon, and here they settled in September 1822 in the Casa Saluzzi, in a suburb of the city named Albaro: Byron occupying one wing of the palace and the Gamba family the other.

This was the man whom Lady Blessington earnestly desired to meet; her desire not being lessened by the fear that he who in general avoided his country people, might decline to become acquainted with her.

Scarcely had she reached her hotel at Genoa, the Alberga della Villa, than taking out her diary she wrote :—

'And am I indeed in the same town with Byron? To-morrow I may perhaps behold him. I never before felt the same impatient longing to see anyone known to me only by his works. I hope he may not be fat as Moore described him; for a fat poet is an anomaly in my opinion. Well well, to-morrow I may know what he is like, and now to bed to sleep away the fatigues of my journey.'

CHAPTER IV

LITTLE time was lost in surmise as to whether
Byron would be gracious to the Blessingtons, or
would refuse to receive them as he had already
done to many acquaintances who had called
on him. For next day, a bright and happy
April day with the gladdening of spring in
the sunny air, Lady Blessington, her husband,
her sister, and Count D'Orsay drove to
the village of Albaro, passing through Genoa,
with its lively crowds of sailors, soldiers, and

civilians, living pictures in themselves; its narrow streets and tall red-hued houses; its magnificent palaces, spacious and sombre; its hanging gardens covering and crowning its rocky heights; and the sight of its sea, a flashing of blue caught in the winding of the ways.

The Earl it will be remembered had known Byron, with whom he was not only desirous of renewing his acquaintance, but to whom he was anxious to introduce his wife. The poet was at this time in his thirty-sixth year. On arriving at the gate of the courtyard Lord Blessington and Count D'Orsay sent in their names and were immediately admitted, when they received a cordial reception from Byron who expressed himself delighted to see a former friend and hoped he might have the pleasure of being presented to Lady Blessington. On this the latter said that she and her sister were in the carriage at the gate.

'Byron then' as the Countess writes 'immediately hurried out into the court, and I who heard the sound of steps, looked through the gate and beheld him approaching quickly without his hat and considerably in advance of the other two gentlemen.

'"You must have thought me quite as illbred and savage as fame reports" said Byron bowing very low "in having permitted your ladyship to remain a quarter of an hour at my gate; but my old friend Lord Blessington is to blame, for I only heard a minute ago that I was so highly honoured. I shall think you do not pardon this apparent rudeness unless you enter my abode, which I entreat you will do" and he offered his hand to assist me to descend from the carriage.

'In the vestibule stood his chasseur in full uniform, with two or three other domestics, and the expression of surprise visible in their countenances evinced that they were not habituated to see their lord display so much cordiality to visitors.'

At first Lady Blessington felt disappointed by the appearance of the poet, because he was unlike the ideal she had imagined of the author of Manfred and Childe Harold. She had expected to find him a dignified, cold, reserved, and haughty individual, resembling the mysterious personages he loved to paint in his works, and with whom he has been so often identified by the world: but nothing she considered could be more different; 'for were I to point out the prominent defect of Lord Byron, I should say it was flippancy and a total want of that natural self-possession and dignity which ought to characterise a man of birth and education.' On reflection however she admitted that most people would be more than satisfied with his appearance and captivated by his manner; for the first was prepossessing and the second cordial.

'His head' she writes 'is peculiarly well-shaped, the forehead high, open, and highly indicative of intellectual power; his eyes are grey and expressive, one is visibly larger than the other; his nose looks handsome in profile, but in front is somewhat clumsy; the eyebrows are well defined and flexible; the mouth is faultless, the upper lip being of Grecian shortness and both as finely chiselled, to use an

artist's phrase, as those of an antique statue.
There is a scornful expression in the latter
feature that does not deteriorate from its
beauty. His chin is large but well-shaped
and not at all fleshy, and finishes well his
face, which is of an oval form. His hair has
already much of silver among its dark brown
curls; its texture is very silky, and although
it retreats from his temples leaving his forehead very bare, its growth at the sides and
back of his head is abundant.

'I have seldom seen finer teeth than Lord
Byron's, and never a smoother or more fair
skin, for though very pale, his is not the
pallor of ill-health. He is so exceedingly
thin that his figure has an almost boyish air;
and yet there is something so striking in his
whole appearance that could not be mistaken
for an ordinary person. I do not think that
I should have observed his lameness, had my
attention not been called to it by his own
visible consciousness of this infirmity — a
consciousness that gives a *gaucherie* to his
movements.'

The residence of the poet was a fine old palace commanding a wide view over olive woods and vineyards that stretched to the bases of the purple Apennines. The saloon into which he led his visitors was high-ceilinged, spacious, and barely furnished, its windows on one side looking into the court-yard and on the other into a stately garden, with orange trees and cedars, terraces and fountains. Into this somewhat sombre room Lady Blessington, her expressive face bright with smiles of triumph and gratification, her exquisite toilette radiant with colour, came as a glow of sunshine. Her host showed every sign of enjoying the company of his visitors.

At first the conversation turned on mutual friends, and then on the number of English people who pestered him with visits, though a great number were unknown to and many of them but slightly acquainted with him. He stated that he steadily refused to receive any but those he really wished to see; as for the others he added 'they avenge themselves by attacking me in every sort of way, and there is no story too improbable for the craving appetites of our slander-loving countrymen.'

On the walls hung a small portrait of his daughter and another of himself, and seeing Lady Blessington looking attentively at the former, he took it from its place and handed it to her. She remarked that the child bore him a strong resemblance which seemed to gratify him.

' I am told she is clever ' he said ' but I hope not ; and above all I hope she is not poetical. The price paid for such advantages, if advantages they be, is such as to make me pray that my child may escape them.'

As he talked to her and her party, Lady Blessington who was a shrewd observer, had opportunities of noticing various characteristics of the poet. ✗ He had the smallest hands she had ever seen with a man, finely-shaped, delicately white, the nails rose-coloured and highly polished so that they resembled delicate pink shells : his voice was clear melodious but somewhat effeminate, and his enunciation so distinct that though his tone was low pitched not a word was lost; whilst his laughter was music itself. Finally she thought he owed less to his clothes than any man of her acquaintance, they being not only old-fashioned but ill-fitting.

When she proposed to end her visit he urged her to stay, and time passed pleasantly. When eventually she rose he warmly expressed the gratification the visit had given him, and Lady Blessington states that she did not doubt his sincerity: not that she claimed any merit to account for his satisfaction, but that she saw he liked hearing news of his old haunts and associates ' and likes also to pass them *en revue*, pronouncing *en passant* opinions in which wit and sly sarcasm are more obvious than good nature. Yet' she adds 'he does not give me the impression that he is ill-natured or malicious, even whilst uttering remarks that imply the presence of these qualities. It appears to me that they proceed from a reckless levity of disposition that renders him incapable of checking the *spirituels* but sarcastic sallies which the possession of a very uncommon

degree of shrewdness, and a still more rare
wit, occasion: and seeing how he amuses
his hearers, he cannot resist the temptation,
although at the expense of many whom he
proposes to like.'

Neither during this visit nor whilst she
remained in Genoa, did Lady Blessington see
the Countess Guiccioli; of whom however
Byron in his subsequent conversations frequently spoke. The young Italian who was
wholly devoted to the poet, led a life of re-
tirement and was seldom seen outside the
grounds of the Casa Saluzzi.

On the day succeeding the visit of Lady
Blessington and her party to the Casa Saluzzi,
Lord Byron presented himself at their hotel,
first sending up two cards in an envelope
as a preliminary to his entrance. They had
just finished *déjeûner*, but the earliness of his
visit did not hinder his welcome. On his
part the poet was brighter and more buoyant
than before.

Lady Blessington told him that as early
as nine that morning she had been to the

flower market, and expressed surprise that the poorest classes bought flowers as if they were the necessaries of life, when Lord Byron fell to praising the people and the city, enumerating amongst its other advantages that it contained so few English either as residents or birds of passage. And as during their previous meeting, so once more did their conversation turn on mutual friends, when Tom Moore amongst others was discussed. Byron spoke more warmly of the Irish bard's attractions as a companion, than of his merits as a poet. 'Lalla Rookh' though beautiful was disappointing to Byron who considered Moore would go down to posterity because of his melodies which were perfect; and he declared he had never been so affected as on hearing Moore sing one of them, particularly 'When first I met thee' which he said made him cry; adding with an arch glance 'but it was after I had drunk a certain portion of very potent white brandy.'

As he laid particular stress on the word *affected* Lady Blessington smiled, when he asked her the cause, on which she told him the story of a lady who on offering her condolence to a poor Irishwoman on the death of her child, stated that she had never been so affected in her life : on hearing which the poor woman, who knew the insincerity of the remark, looked up and said 'Sure thin ma'am that's saying a great deal, for you were always affected.'

All present laughed at this, and then Lady Holland was brought upon the board. Lady Blessington felt surprised by his flippancy in talking of those for whom he expressed a regard, understanding which he remarked laughingly that he feared he should lose her good opinion by his frankness, but that when the fit was on him he could not help saying what he thought, though he often repented it when too late.

Throughout his conversation he continually censured his own country. His friends told him Count D'Orsay had during his visit to London kept a journal in which he dealt freely with the follies of society. This interested

Byron much, and led him to ask permission
to read the manuscript, which D'Orsay freely
gave him. Throughout this visit which lasted
for two hours, he said very little of his own
works ; and Lady Blessington thought he had
far less pretension than any literary man of her
acquaintance, and not the slightest shade of
pedantry.

Before leaving he promised to dine with them
on the following Thursday ; theirs being, as he
assured them, the first invitation to dinner he
had accepted for two years.

On returning to his palazzo, Byron sat down
and wrote to Moore 'I have just seen some
friends of yours who paid me a visit yesterday,
which in honour of them and of you, I returned
to-day; as I reserve my bearskin and teeth, and
paws and claws for our enemies. . . . Your allies,
whom I found very agreeable personages, are
Milor Blessington and *épouse*, travelling with a
very handsome companion in the shape of a
'French count' (to use Farquhar's phrase in
the 'Beau's Stratagem ') who has all the air of a
Cupidon déchaîné, and is one of the few specimens

I have seen of our ideal of a Frenchman *before* the Revolution—an old friend with a new face upon whose like I never thought that we should look again. Miladi seems highly literary, to which and your honour's acquaintance with the family I attribute the pleasure of having seen them. She is also very pretty, even in a morning, a species of beauty on which the sun of Italy does not shine so frequently as the chandelier.'

Having read the journal of Count D'Orsay, in whom he was already interested, he returned it to Lord Blessington remarking that it was 'a very extraordinary production and of a most melancholy truth in all that regards high life in England.'

'I know' he continues 'or know personally most of the personages and societies which he describes ; and after reading his remarks have the sensation fresh upon me as if I had seen them yesterday. I would however plead in behalf of some few exceptions, which I will mention by-and-by. The most singular thing is, *how* he should have penetrated *not* the *facts* but the *mystery* of English *ennui*, at two-and-twenty. I was about the same age when I made the same discovery in almost precisely the same circles—for there is scarcely a person whom I did not see nightly or daily, and was acquainted more or 'less intimately with most of them—but I never could have discovered it so well, *Il faut être Français* to effect this.

'But he ought also to have been in the country during the hunting season, with "a select party of distinguished guests" as the papers term it. He ought to have seen the gentlemen after dinner (on the hunting days) and the *soirée* ensuing thereupon—and the women looking as if they had hunted, or rather been hunted : and I could have wished that he had been at a dinner in town, which I recollect at Lord Cowper's small but select, and composed of the most amusing people.-

'Altogether your friend's journal is a very formidable production. Alas our dearly beloved countrymen have only discovered that they are tired and not that they are tiresome: and I suspect that the communication of the latter

unpleasant verity will not be better received
than truths usually are. I have read the whole
with great attention and instruction—I am too
good a patriot to say *pleasure*—at least I
won't say so whatever I may think.'

Now the fact that Byron was to dine with the
Blessingtons on a certain evening, having got
noised abroad probably through the servants,
the English residents in the Albergo della Villa
and other hotels assembled in the courtyard,
on the stairs, and in the corridors to see him
arrive and greet him with a stolid British stare.
Fortunately for his hosts he was not in a
humour to resent this intrusion, but appeared
in good spirits as he entered their *salon*, for
when in good humour he set down the stares
and comments of his country-people whenever
they met him, to their admiration; but when
worried or depressed he resented them as impertinent curiosity, caused by the scandalous
histories he believed were circulated regarding
him. No sooner was he in the room than he
began to talk of himself though not of his
poems : his animated countenance changing its

expression with the subjects that excited his feelings.

Lady Blessington thought it strange that he should speak to recent acquaintances with such perfect abandon on subjects which even friends would consider too delicate for discussion. His family affairs were debated and details given. He declared he was in ignorance of why his wife had parted from him, but suspected it was through the ill-natured interference of others, and that he had left no means untried to effect a reconciliation. He added with some bitterness that a day would come when he would be avenged, for 'I feel' he said 'that I shall not live long, and when the grave has closed over me what must she feel.'

Afterwards he went on to praise the mental and personal qualities of his wife, when Lady Blessington ventured to say that the appreciation he expressed somewhat contradicted the sarcasms supposed to refer to Lady Byron in his works. At this the poet shook his head and his face lighted with a smile as he explained that what he had written was meant to spite and vex her at a time when he was wounded and irritated at her refusing to receive or answer his letters. He was sorry for what he had penned regarding her, but 'notwithstanding this regret and all his good resolutions to avoid similar sins, he might on renewed provocation recur to the same vengeance, though he allowed it was petty and unworthy of him.'

In all his conversations this singular man whose character was a mass of contradictions, delighted in confessing his faults: how he could bear to have them recognised by another, remained to be proved. Lady Blessington shrewdly enough remarks that those who show the greatest frankness in admitting their errors, are precisely the people who resent their detection by others. She did not think Byron insincere in commenting on his defects, for his perception was too keen to leave him unaware of them; and his desire of proving his perception was too great not to give proof of this power by self analysis. It appeared to her as if he

were more ready to own than to correct his
faults; and that he considered his candour in
acknowledging them an *amende honorable*.

'There is an indescribable charm to me at
least' she writes 'in hearing people to whom
genius of the highest order is ascribed, indulge
in egotistical conversation; more especially
when they are free from affectation, and all are
more or less so when talking of self, a subject
on which they speak *con amore*. It is like
reading their diaries by which we learn more
of the individuals than by any other means.'

At dinner that evening the poet was in
high spirits and enjoyed himself heartily.
Turning to his hostess he hoped she was not
shocked by seeing him eating so much 'but
the truth is' he added 'that for several months
I have been following a most abstemious *régime*,
living almost entirely on vegetables; and now
that I see a good dinner I cannot resist temptation, though to-morrow I shall suffer for my
gourmandise as I always do when I indulge in
luxuries.' This he added was a *jour de fête*
when he would eat, drink, and make merry.

✗ The scheme of living which he followed consisted not only in dieting himself on vegetables, drinking vinegar, taking medicine in excess, but at times in enduring pangs of hunger, by means of which he hoped to master a natural tendency to stoutness, and by keeping thin to preserve that finer outline of face and symmetry of form which gave interest to his appearance and youthfulness to his figure. ✗

He explained to his friends that no choice was left him but to sacrifice his body to his mind: that if he lived as others, he would not only be ill, but would lose his intellectual faculties. To eat animal food, he argued, was to engender animal appetites; as proof of which he instanced the manner in which boxers are fed: whilst to live on fish and vegetables was to support without pampering existence.

He took evident pride in arriving at a result which cost him so much pain; and with a boyish air would ask 'Don't you think I get thinner?' or again 'Did you ever see anyone so thin as I am who was not ill?' One day Lady Blessington assuming a grave face and a serious air assured him she believed that his living so continually on fish resulted in his fondness for and his skill in swimming ; a theory which he was ready to admit, and would have discoursed on, if, unable to command herself, she had not burst out laughing, a proceeding that at first puzzled him, but in which he joined a second later saying,—

'Well Miladi, after this hour never accuse me any more of mystifying: you did take me in until you laughed.'

This desired condition of thinness was really obtained at the expense of his health. He obstinately resisted the advice of medical men and friends, who assured him of his folly in continuing austerities that were certainly undermining his constitution, which would have no power of recovery if once attacked by illness: a prediction not long afterwards fulfilled.

It was on the second day after Byron had dined with the Blessingtons, that news was

brought them of an event destined to influence the lives of two at least of the party,
though unforeseen by them. Lady Blessington
and her husband were in the *salon* of their
hotel when they saw a courier covered
with dust ride into the courtyard. A presentiment of evil seized her, as she relates,
a presentiment which was verified a moment
later when a letter was handed the Earl
stating that his only legitimate son and heir,
Viscount Mountjoy was dead. The boy then
about ten years old had been ailing for some
time; but as the Countess writes 'although
long prepared for this melancholy event, it
has fallen on us as heavily as if we counted
on his days being lengthened. Poor dear
Mountjoy, he expired on the 26th of March,
and Carlo Forte the courier, reached this from
London in eight days. Well may it be said
that bad news travels quickly.'

This intelligence fell like a shadow on the
party for a little while, during which Byron
showed the greatest kindness and feeling towards Lord Blessington. 'There is a gentle-

ness and almost womanly softness in his manner towards him that is peculiarly pleasing to witness' Lady Blessington writes. Her favourite horse Mameluke having arrived, the whole party rode to Nervi a few days later, the poet acting as their cicerone. He was neither a good nor a bold rider, though he had much pretensions to horsemanship and when mounted must have presented an extraordinary figure; for his horse was covered with trappings, whilst the saddle was *à la hussarde*, its holsters bristling with pistols. The rider wore nankeen jacket and trousers a trifle shrunk from washing, the jacket embroidered, the waist short, the back narrow, three rows of buttons in front; a black satin stock clasping his neck; on his head a dark blue velvet cap with a shade, a rich gold tassel hanging from the crown; nankeen gaiters, and a pair of blue spectacles.

Knowing Genoa and its surroundings he pointed out sites of surpassing beauty, but a certain indifference he exhibited towards their charm surprised Lady Blessington, on expressing which he said laughingly 'I suppose you expected me to explode into some enthusiastic exclamations on the sea, the scenery etc., such as poets indulge in, or rather are supposed to indulge in ; but the truth is I hate cant of every kind, and the cant of the love of nature as much as any other.' 'So' she comments 'to avoid the appearance of one affectation he assumes another, that of not admiring.'

His views regarding art brought her greater surprise. He liked music without knowing anything of it as a science, of which he was glad, as he feared a perfect knowledge would rob music of half its charms. 'At present I only know' he said 'that a plaintive air softens, and a lively one cheers me. Martial music renders me brave, and voluptuous music disposes me to be luxurious, even effeminate. Now were I skilled in the science I should become fastidious ; and instead of yielding to the fascination of sweet sounds, I should be analysing, or criticising, or connoisseurshipising (to use a word of my own making) instead of simply enjoying them as at present. In the same way I never would study botany. 1 don't want to know why certain flowers please me; enough for me that they do, and I leave to those who have no better occupation, the analyses of the sources of their pleasure, which I can enjoy without the useless trouble.'

His love of flowers amounted to a passion, and this and his charity were two beautiful traits in his character; for he never refused to give when asked, and always gave with a gentleness and kindness that enhanced the giving; so that the poor knew and loved him and came to him in their needs and sorrows. Perfumes also had a strong effect upon him and as he said, often made him quite sentimental.

Byron seemed as delighted with the companionship of the Blessingtons as they were with his, and he was continually dining, or riding with them, writing to or calling on them, or sitting for his portrait to D'Orsay in their *salon*, and this close association enabled the Countess to notice many traits in him before unsuspected. Now he comes to drink tea with her after dinner, and being animated tells stories of his London life, gossips about acquaintances and mimics the people he describes, ridiculing their vanities and telling their secrets. He delighted in hearing what was passing in the world of fashion, and his correspondents in London kept him *au courant* of its scandals. One day Lady Blessington suggested that attention to such trifles was unworthy of a mind like his, when he answered that the trunk of an elephant which could lift a great weight did not disdain a small one, and he confessed to loving a little scandal as he believed all English people did.

Another day he calls upon her, fuming with indignation because of an attack on him, first made in an American paper and afterwards copied into Galignani, from the effects of which his temper did not recover for several days; for never was man so sensitive to the censures and opinions of those whom he neither knew nor respected; whilst at the same time he showed a want of perception and disregard to the feelings of others; a not uncommon combination, which is the result of egotism.

Again he rides out with her and speaks of his expedition to Greece, and jests at the intention of his turning soldier; but his laughter is not genuine enough to cover the seriousness with which he viewed the project. On this his companion held out the hope that he would return full of glory in having fought in the cause of freedom, so that his country would feel proud of him; but at that prospect he mournfully shook his head, saying he had more than once dreamt that he would die in Greece, and continually had a presentiment that such would be the case.

Asked why he did not then give up all idea of the expedition, he replied that he would yield himself to the dictates of fate; he had always believed his life would not be long; he did not wish to live to old age; and he desired to rest his bones in a country hallowed by the recollections of youth and dreams of happiness never realised.

'A grassy bed in Greece and a grey stone to mark the spot' he said 'would please me more than a marble tomb in Westminster Abbey, an honour which if I were to die in England, I suppose could not be refused to me: for though my compatriots were unwilling to let me live in peace in the land of my fathers, they would not, kind souls, object to my ashes resting in peace among those of the poets of my country.'

Poor Byron, though he made immense allowances for the hypocrisy, narrowness, and uncharitableness of his countrymen, he failed to foresee the fierceness of a chastity that denied to his bust a niche in the Abbey.

Not only did he believe in fate, but he placed faith in supernatural appearances, in lucky and unlucky days, would never undertake any act of importance on Fridays, and had the greatest horror of letting bread fall, spilling salt, or breaking mirrors. Whenever he spoke of ghosts as he was fond of doing, 'he assumes,' as Lady Blessington writes 'a grave and mysterious air, and he has told me some extraordinary stories relative to Mr Shelley who, he assures me, had an implicit belief in ghosts.' The fact that she did not share his belief in the supernatural, seemed to offend him, and he said that she must therefore believe herself wiser than he, 'and he left me' she tells us 'evidently displeased at my want of superstition.'

One delicious evening in May when the blue of the sea and the balm of its breath tempted the Blessingtons to set out on a boating excursion, Byron felt inclined to accept their invitation to accompany them, 'but when we were about to embark' narrates Lady Blessington 'a superstitious presentiment induced him to give up the water party, which set us all laughing at him, which he bore very well, although he half smiled and said "No, no, good folk, you shall not laugh me out of my superstition, even though you may think me a fool for it."'

Two days later he wrote her a note in

which occurs the sentence 'I did well to avoid the water party—*why* is a mystery which is not less to be wondered at than all my other mysteries.'

After a stay of about six weeks in Genoa the Blessingtons, having seen all the city and its environs had to show, began to make preparations to resume their journey which they now decided was to end in Naples. The prospect of losing such pleasant neighbours and friends was displeasing to Byron who warmly urged them to remain until he had started for Greece. The force and frequency with which he returned to the subject was flattering, and the pouting sulkiness, like a child crossed in a whim, with which he resented their refusal, was amusing. His displeasure increasing, he declared he would never dine with them again at their hotel, now he saw how little disposed they were to gratify him; when his hostess with some dignity declared that had she known his dining with them was considered a sacrifice by him, she never would have invited him; on which reproof he seemed a little ashamed of his petulance.

Then he took them to see an extremely picturesque but slightly dilapidated villa named Il Paradiso, situated near his own palace, which he suggested they should rent. Lady Blessington admired it greatly, when the poet taking a pencil wrote the following lines :—

> 'Beneath Blessington's eyes
> The reclaimed paradise
> Should be free as the former from evil ;
> But if the new Eve
> For an apple should grieve,
> What mortal would not play the devil?'

Handing her this he said 'In future times people will come to see Il Paradiso where Byron wrote an impromptu on his country-woman ; thus our names will be associated when we have long ceased to exist.' To this Lady Blessington added in her diary 'And heaven only knows to how many commentaries so simple an incident may hereafter give rise.'

Eventually the Blessingtons decided not to

take the villa, and the day of their departure from Genoa was fixed. Byron, who foresaw how much he should miss their pleasant company, became graver in his manner and continually dwelt on his journey to Greece. If he outlived the campaign, he declared he would write two poems on the subject, one an epic and the other a burlesque in which none would be spared, himself least of all: for if he took liberties with them he took greater freedoms with himself, and he thought they ought to bear with him out of consideration for his impartiality.

This he said when making one of those efforts at gaiety that only showed more clearly the underlying sadness with which he viewed his projected expedition. 'I have made as many sacrifices to liberty' he remarked one day 'as most people of my age, and the one I am about to undertake is not the least, though probably it will be the last: for with my broken health and the chances of war, Greece will most likely terminate my mortal career. I like Italy, its climate, its customs, and above all its freedom from cant of every kind, which is the *primum mobile* of England ; therefore it is no slight sacrifice of comfort to give up the tranquil life I lead here, and break through the ties I have formed, to engage in a cause for the successful result of which I have no very sanguine hopes.'

And then he added that though he feared his hearer might think him more superstitious than ever, he would repeat that he had a presentiment he should die in Greece. 'I hope it may be in action' he continued, 'for that would be a good finish to a very *triste* existence, and I have a horror of death-bed scenes ; but as I have not been famous for my luck in life, most probably I shall not have more in the manner of my death, and I may draw my last sigh, not on the field of glory, but on the bed of disease. I very nearly died when I was in Greece in my youth ; perhaps as things have turned out it would have been well if I had ; I should have lost nothing and the world very little, and I should have escaped many cares, for God knows I have had enough of one kind or another : but I am getting gloomy, and looking either back or forward is not calculated to enliven me. One of the reasons why I quiz my friends in conversation is, that it keeps me from thinking of myself.'

As the days passed he frequently expressed a wish to return to England, if only for a few weeks, before departing for Greece; but though he was lord of himself in all ways, he never, from want of firmness of determination, put this desire into effect. His principal reason for wishing to visit his native land was to hold his little daughter for once in his arms, and if possible to see and become reconciled to his wife, who had refused all explanation of the cause of her separation from him, all attempt at reconciliation, who had returned his letters unopened, and who had remained silent whilst his enemies attributed various and contradictory phases of vileness to him. That which influenced him most in preventing him from visiting England was the fear that his wife would continue her heartless conduct towards him, that his child would be prevented from seeing him, and that any step his affection might prompt him to take in asserting his right to see her, would be misrepresented as an act of barbarous tyranny and persecution towards mother and child, when he would be driven from England more vilified and with greater ignominy than on his separation.

'Such is my idea of the justice of public opinion in England' he said 'and with such woeful experiences as I have had, can you wonder that I dare not encounter the annoyances I have detailed. But if I live and return from Greece with something better and higher than the reputation or glory of a poet, opinions may change, as the successful are always judged favourably of in our country: my laurels may cover my faults better than the bays have done, and give a totally different reading to my thoughts, words, and actions.'

Before his friends left he wished to buy Lady Blessington's favourite horse Mameluke; and to sell his yacht to Lord Blessington.

On first seeing Mameluke, Byron had expressed great admiration for him. Thinking him a docile easily-managed beast, he had asked innumerable questions about him, and subsequently requested as a favour that his owner would sell him ; the poet stating he would take Mameluke to Greece, for with so steady a charger he would feel confidence in action, and that he would never part with him.

Lady Blessington who was fond of all animals, was much attached to this horse, and was reluctant to sell him : she knew moreover she would have great difficulty in replacing him : yet her good nature prompting her, she consented to Byron's frequent entreaties and agreed to part with Mameluke.

The horse had cost a hundred guineas, but when the hour of payment came, Byron wrote to say that he could not afford to give more than eighty pounds 'as I have to undergo con-. siderable expense at the present time.' No wonder Lady Blessington writes ' How strange to beg and entreat to have the horse resigned to him, and then name a price less than he cost.'

In openly dwelling on his own faults as was his habit, Byron had said that in addition to others, avarice was now established; and again when stating that his friend Hobhouse had pointed out many imperfections of character to him, the poet continued 'I could have told him of some more which he had not discovered, for even then avarice had made itself strongly felt in my nature.' Whilst at Genoa the Blessingtons had frequent opportunities of noting his love for money; for in making the rounds of the city with them, he would occasionally express his delight at some specimen of art or article of furniture until he had inquired the price, when he shrank back at thought of the expense, and congratulated himself on requiring no such luxuries.

Before leaving they were to have a further proof of this peculiarity. As he was going to Greece he had no need for his yacht, the *Bolivar*, which as already stated he wished

Lord Blessington to buy. The boat was luxuriously furnished, and its couches of Genoese velvet and its marble baths particularly pleased Lady Blessington, who was, however, more attracted by the fact that he had written several of his poems on board. It was therefore agreed that they should buy the yacht, the price of which was left for Mr Barry, Byron's friend and banker, to determine : but when the latter fixed a sum, Byron demanded a higher figure, which the extravagant Irish peer gave without condescending to bargain. 'The poet is certainly fond of money' comments Lady Blessington.

On the 27th of May Byron dined with his hospitable friends, 'our last dinner together for heaven knows how long, perhaps for ever' writes the hostess. None of those who sat round the board was gay; Byron least of all. Looking paler and thinner than ever, he fell into silence continually, from which he roused himself to assume an appearance of gaiety. Once more he spoke of his expedition to· Greece and wished he had not pledged himself to go ; adding that having promised, he must now fulfil his engagement. Then he eagerly grasped at an idea held out to him of paying a visit before he left to his friends when they reached Naples, and sailing in the bay on board the *Bolivar :* and with this pleasant hope he left them for that night.

Four evenings later came a time of trial for all of them when the poet, pale and dejected, entered the *salon* to say farewell. In this melancholy hour the presentiment that he would never return from his expedition and that they would never meet again seemed to strengthen to certainty. 'Here we are now all together' he said sadly 'but when and where shall we meet again? I have a sort of boding that we see each other for the last time ; as something tells me I shall never again return from Greece.'

Then unable to control his voice any longer he leaned his head on the arm of the sofa on which he and Lady Blessington were seated, and bursting into tears sobbed for some time in the fulness of bitter feeling. The whole party were impressed and moved and the hostess especially, ever tender and sympathetic, was overcome] by grief.

Presently, by one of those strange and sudden transitions of his character, Byron drying his tears, once more reproached her for not remaining in Genoa until he sailed for Greece, again showing some pique, and referring sarcastically to his nervousness by way of excusing his emotion. Later he softened once more and gave them all some little present by which they might remember him in years to come; to one a book, to another a print of his bust by Bartolini, and to Lady Blessington a copy of his Armenian Grammar which contained notes in his own writing. In return he asked for some souvenir, something she had worn that he might keep; on which she took a ring from her finger and gave it to him.

Byron was touched and gratified, and on the impulse of the moment took from his stock and presented to her a pin bearing a small cameo of Napoleon, which the poet said had long been his companion.

When the final words came to be said his lips quivered, his voice became inarticulate, and tears rushed into his eyes. His parting was full of melancholy.

That night Lady Blessington, heavy of heart and oppressed by nervous fear, wrote in her diary :—

'Should his presentiment be realised, and we indeed meet no more, I shall never cease to remember him with kindness; the very idea that I shall not see him again, over-powers me with sadness, and makes me forget many defects which had often disenchanted me with him. Poor Byron. I will not allow myself to think that we have met for the last time: although he has infected us all by his superstitious forebodings.'

Though they were to see him no more, they were to hear from him again before they left Genoa, for next morning came a note which contained the following words :—

'MY DEAR LADY BLESSINGTON,—I am *superstitious* and have recollected that memorials with a *point* are of less fortunate augury: I will therefore request you to accept instead of the *pin*, the enclosed chain which is of so slight a value that you need not hesitate. As you wished for something *worn* I can only say that it has been worn oftener and longer than any other. It is of Venetian manufacture, and the only peculiarity about it is, that it could only be obtained at or from Venice. At Genoa they have none of the same kind.

'I also enclose a ring which I would wish Alfred to keep, it is too large to *wear;* but it is formed of *lava* and so far adapted to the fire of his years and character. You will perhaps have the goodness to acknowledge the receipt of this note, and send back the pin (for good luck's sake) which I shall value much more for having been a night in your custody.'

CHAPTER V

First Sight of Naples—The City Crowds—A
Magnificent Palace—Entertaining—Sir William
Gell—My Lord's Extravagance—The Building of
a Fairy Palace—Lord Blessington returns to
Italy—Travelling in Former Times—The Inn at
Borghetto—Life in the Palazzo Belvedere—Young
Mathews as a Mimic—Amateur Theatricals—
Above the Bay.

FROM Genoa the Blessington party travelled
to Florence where they stayed about a month,
then visited Siena and Rome which in the
month of July they found intolerably hot,
and thence to Naples their destination.

Reaching this wonderful city by one of the
steep hills in its background, they stopped
their carriages to look down with delight on
the labyrinth of streets, tortuous, quaint, and
narrow, and vivid coloured in the glow of the
sun ; on the palaces surrounded by terraces and
gardens, on innumerable churches with domes

and bell towers, and above all on the bay, serene and sunny, whose unbroken blue was scarce darker than the sky, whose islands three, floated verdant and phantasmal beyond, whose opposite shores were dotted by villages white in the glare, and lined by groves of orange and lemon that descended to the sea.

Here was the city of their dreams, the city they had travelled far to see, the first sight of which held them speechless. And if by day 'twas wonderful, by night and moonlight it was magical : here they resolved to stay. At first they hired a suite of rooms in the hotel Grand Bretagna, whilst looking out for a suitable residence in which to settle. The life of the city surged around them ; and all things—the crowds with their volcanic gaiety, the shops full of antiquities, the market-places, the quarters of the ear-ringed red-capped fishermen, the religious processions and church ceremonies—were new with a newness that brought delight.

At night when refreshing breezes crept up from the bay, mirthful as children free for a holiday, they went into the streets to mix amongst the people and make one of them; passing the *cafés* and ice shops with their marble tables and brilliant lights; ' the tobacco shops with their crowds; the portable barrows or *bottegi* with their canopies of striped lawn, the gorgeous colours of their ill-drawn pictorial designs, their bright-hued paper lanterns, where were sold lemonade, ice water, or *sorbetto*, macaroni hot and savoury smelling, water melons mines of golden fruit in green rinds, pomegranates scarlet and juicy, *frittura*, shell fish, gingerbread fantastically shaped, and pictures of the madonna and saints. Then forever above the din of those who cried their wares, and the indistinct murmur of crowds, came the sounds of guitars and the voices of singers as they passed a corner or came through the archway of an alley; or the high-pitched prayers of a beggar; or the ringing laughter of women's voices, all sounds perhaps suddenly hushed as a priest and his acolyte passed through a lane of kneeling figures, bearing the host to one dying.

On the Chiaja in the evening cool, carriages drove backwards and forwards, in which were seated dark-complexioned women with glowing eyes and raven hair, fanning themselves languorously, gesticulating, smiling.

In the Mole down by the sea, and full of the brine of its breath, the crowds were chiefly composed of brown-legged, bare-armed sailors, with their wives whose full throats were clasped by amber and coral. Here a young man whose voice was sweet as music, whose face was like to Cæsar on a coin, recited Tasso's 'Gerusalemme' to groups of men and women whom he stirred and swayed, and whose silence was broken only by bursts of applause.

Further down were two who sang duets, love songs, and songs of the sea, accompanying themselves on their guitars; whilst in another direction Punch, a genuine native of this clime, played pranks and jested wittily to crowds who watched his antics by the glare of oil lamps, and answered his quips with peals of laughter.

And not far from him, standing on a chair,

his voice raised, his gestures imploring, a scarce heeded monk called sinners to repentance.

After having looked at half the palaces in Naples and its environs, the Blessingtons at last hired as their residence the Palazzo Belvedere at Vomero, a princely building situated on a hill that gave it a magnificent prospect, and surrounded by beautiful gardens that overlooked the bay. A stately archway led through spacious pleasure grounds planted with palms and oranges and sweet-smelling shrubs, to the palace which formed three sides of a square, the fourth being filled by an arcade. In the centre of the courtyard was a marble fountain mellowed by time to an amber hue. A pillared colonnade extended in front; the windows of the five reception rooms opened on a raised terrace with marble balustrades, at one end of which was an open-arched pavilion that looked out upon the 'happy fields' lying at the base of a fore-ground of descending vineyards; beyond lay Vesuvius, the mountain itself a purple height against transparent blue; and below, slept the bay, a scene and source of undying beauty, of unending delight.

Interiorly the palace was spacious and lofty, the ceilings painted and gilded, the floors of marble; pillars of Oriental alabaster supporting archways; statues and pictures filling rooms and galleries. Before taking possession of the palace, Lady Blessington added to the cumberous sofas, the gilt chairs, the tables of malachite and agate with which it was already furnished, curtains, carpets, rugs and various articles which gave comfort to its somewhat chilling splendour.

Then their English banker living in Naples 'a most gentlemanly and obliging personage' engaged Neopolitan servants for them; when their mistress became acquainted with a system of housekeeping different from any she had known before, and one which saved a world of trouble and imposition. This being that an agreement was entered into with the cook to furnish all meals according to the number of dishes at a stipulated price per head, each guest invited being paid for at the same rate.

At the end of each week a bill, resembling that of an hotel, except that it contained no separate items, was presented by the cook and checked by the *maître d'hotel.*

Being now established in the Palazzo Belvedere, Lady Blessington heartily congratulated herself on the comforts of a private house after spending eleven months in hotels. Dear to her was the comfort of 'being sure of meeting no strangers on the stairs; no intruders in the ante-rooms; of hearing no slappings of doors; no knocking about of trunks and imperials; no cracking of whips of postilions; no vociferations of couriers; and above all of not having our olfactory organs disgusted by the abominable odour of cigars. 'Surely' she says ' an exemption from such annoyances after an endurance of them for nearly a year, is in itself a subject for satisfaction ; but to have secured such an abode as this palazzo, is indeed a cause for thankfulness.'

Lady Blessington and her party now gave themselves up to sight - seeing and to entertaining. Scarcely a day passed that some foreigner of distinction, or some Englishman of position passing through or visiting Naples, did not dine with them; whilst she was ever ready to welcome them to her *salon* in the evenings. Their hospitality was widespread and warm-hearted.

Now it was Prince Buttera who dined with them; the Prince once a plain soldier of fortune having gained the hand and with it the wealth and title of a princess and an heiress who had fallen in love with him; then it was Millingen the antiquary who stayed some days with and gave them lectures on numismatics; again their guests were the Duke of Roccoromano and Prince Ischittelli; or Count Paul Lieven, a Russian who spoke English fluently, or Herschel the English astronomer, and Hamilton the English minister, or the Duc de Fitzjames, or Lord Howden, or Westmacott the young sculptor, or Lord Dudley who was eccentric, but was not considered mad, owing to his possessing fifty thousand a year; or Lord Ashley on his way to Sicily, or Lord Guilford returning from Corfu.

Then they were entertained by Harry Neale, admiral of the English Fleet stationed in the bay; or were conducted by night to the observatory at Capo di Monte by Herschel himself, where they viewed the stars; or were invited to dinner by the Archbishop of Tarentum, a · white-haired picturesque prelate, suspended from his office for dabbling in revolutions, who wished them to meet Son Altesse Royale the Prince Gustave of Mechlenbourg; or were taken by Lord Dudley to see the beautiful grounds of the Villa Gallo; or ascended Vesuvius and spent a day at Pompeii under the guidance of the learned Sir William Gell, leading in all a joyous life, unknown to care.

One of their most frequent guests and intimate friends was Sir William Gell the archæologist and traveller who had published many learned works and had in his day played the part of a courtier; he having accompanied Queen Charlotte, the unhappy wife of George the Fourth, in her journey to Italy, as one of her chamberlains. From 1820 he lived in Italy, having a house in Rome and another

in Naples where 'surrounded by books, drawings and maps, with a guitar and two or
three dogs' he received numbers of distinguished visitors. For years previous to his
death he suffered from gout and rheumatism,
but though his hands were swollen to a
great size with chalkstones he handled a
pencil or pen with great delicacy and sketched
with remarkable rapidity and accuracy.

In Lady Blessington's *salon* where he was
ever welcome, he rolled himself about in his
chair, being unable to walk, telling. her droll
anecdotes, talking on archæological subjects,
or playing on a rough Greek double flute as an
accompaniment to a dog whom he had taught
to sing in a wonderful manner. It was he
who probably inspired her with a desire to
see the Pyramids, for she talked much of
journeying to Egypt about this time, though
the project was never accomplished.

Sir William Gell was not the only resident
who served to make Lady Blessington's stay
agreeable ; for at this period there had settled
here a group of well-known individuals—many

of them her own countrymen who formed a delightful social circle.

Amongst them was Sir William Drummond, at one time British Envoy Extraordinary and Minister Plenipotentiary to the King of the two Sicilies; a learned man and a prolific author, a philosopher and a poet who so far outraged philosophy and followed poetry as to marry when advanced in life, a gay young wife; who spent his immense wealth freely, dressed magnificently, and graciously smiled upon her lap-dog and her husband's secretary. The Abbé Campbell an ecclesiastic of the old school was another person of note: rotund in person, purple-visaged, snuff-smeared, and bull-necked; an Irishman, a wit, a lover of good wine, a satirist, who though devoid of the advantages of birth or breeding or culture, could boast of the friendship of kings and princes, and exercised a mysterious influence over the governments of great countries. Humorous as he was, he was not excelled in that quality by another Hibernian, Doctor Quinn, who had a large practice amongst the

English residents and visitors; a man ever ready with repartee, full of humanity. hearty and most hospitable.

Scarce less a favourite amongst all was Doctor Reilly, likewise Irish; a retired navy surgeon, wild-spirited, who in his day was concerned with strange romances in which rope ladders and convent walls formed conspicuous scenic effects: but who now had settled down to matrimony which brought wealth. Never was man more jocose, especially at his table round which he delighted to gather his friends not less than twice a week; and many rare passages of arms were exchanged between himself and the Abbé.

Then came a dear and lovable old man General Wade from Westmeath, who by some strange turn of fortune's wheel was Commandant of the Castello D'Ovo, and who rejoiced in entertaining his friends, not alone with the pleasures he set before them, but by the stories which he told them; harmless, full of frolic, now and then throwing

side lights upon his own adventures and the
bravery of his deeds.

The Hon. Keppel Craven, Lord Craven's
son was another of this group, a particular
friend of Sir William Gell with whom he had
acted as chamberlain to George the Fourth's
wife when she had set out on her travels,
but whose service he left at Naples. A
scholar, a musician, an amateur actor and
something of an artist, he was always warmly
welcomed at the Palazzo Belvedere.

And not least of this group was Captain
Hesse, the son of a Prussian banker who
had obtained a commission in an English
regiment, whose handsome appearance had
caused the Princess Charlotte of Wales
when a girl, to smile at him encouragingly
as he gaily rode past her window, and later
to enter into a correspondence with and give
him her portrait.

With these and others who came and went,
the residents of the Palazzo Belvedere were
well entertained. But scarcely had his family
been settled at Naples, than Lord Blessington

found it necessary to return to England and subsequently to Ireland that he might arrange some pressing business. Whilst travelling with a retinue of servants through France and Italy, hiring suites of apartments in expensive hotels and entertaining largely, he yet kept up his town house in St James's Square, and his country house in Mountjoy Forest.

This expenditure outran his income, his estates being already hampered by mortgages ; and large sums of ready money were raised from time to time on his property ; such paltry considerations by no means interfering with his characteristic extravagance. Nay even at this time he thought of erecting a castle in Mountjoy Forest, instead of the roomy rambling old house in which he resided when he visited Ireland for a few weeks in the hunting season.

He was full of this idea when in London in the summer of 1823, and whilst one day visiting his friend Charles Mathews the actor, was struck by some plans and designs he saw hanging on the walls of his rooms. The actor proudly explained that these had been drawn by his son Charles, who had been articled for four years to Augustus Pugin the architect, and was now about to start for himself. With his habitual good nature Lord Blessington there and then declared he would give the lad an opportunity of making his name in the profession he had selected, by letting him erect Mountjoy Castle. The elder Mathews who was delighted at the project offered his profuse thanks when the Earl and the actor parted. Young Charles had been educated at Merchant Taylor's School and afterwards under a private tutor at Clapham. It had been his father's intention to make a clergyman of the boy, who however showed no inclination to become a parson. Handsome and graceful in person, he was quick and vivacious in temperament, sunny natured, full of tact, with a rich inheritance of varied talent, and a gentleness withal that won him the admiration and love of those who knew him.

To him Lord Blessington's promise was a source of excitement and delight, which was heightened a couple of weeks later by the receipt of the following letter addressed by the Earl to Charles Mathews the elder:—

'If you like the idea send him (Charles) off forthwith to Liverpool or Holyhead, from which places steamers go, and by the Derry mail he will be here (with resting a day in Dublin) in five days: but he must lose no time in setting off. I will bring him back in my carriage.'

To this was added in a postscript an invitation, which it was hoped might tempt the elder Mathews to visit a country in whose capital he had in his youth, performed without credit to himself.

'I suppose' it said 'it would be utterly useless my asking you to come with Charles; but if you wish to spend a week in one of the most beautiful spots in Ireland, eat the best vension, Highland mutton and rabbits, and drink the best claret in Ireland, this is the place: and you would be received with undivided applause, and I would give you some comical dresses for your kit.'

The invitation was no sooner received than it was accepted on behalf of the son who was soon ready to start for Ireland but had to wait a couple of days before beginning his journey as the mail-coach was full : whilst a similar occurence detained him in Dublin. Once arrived at Mountjoy Forest he began what he terms the grand project, and revelled in the delightful occupation of building castles in the air. The Earl was enthusiastic regarding his scheme. As Mathews relates in his autobiography ' fifty different plans were furnished, and fifty different alterations were suggested, till the time ran away and we were not much further advanced than when we started. Lord Blessington was absorbed in his grand idea, and went mad over the details. Suggestion upon suggestion and alteration upon alteration succeeded each other hour by hour; but nothing daunted I followed all his caprices with patience and good-humour, and even derived amusement from his flights of fancy.'

The fact was, as this shrewd young man soon discovered, that his chief charm lay in his acquiescence with my lord's whims. He had already been furnished with plans on a magnificent scale for a castle by Wyatt, who would not permit a suggestion or allow an alteration, a despotism that by no means suited the Earl, who really wanted to design the residence and to suggest the arrangements, and merely required someone smart enough to put his plans in shape and carry out his practical details. 'I am just the person for him' says Mathews 'ardent as himself, and rather delighting in, than objecting to the constant exercise for ingenuity his exuberant conceptions afforded me, and we laboured capitally together.'

In this way a couple of months were pleasantly passed, when after much deliberation and innumerable changes, an appropriate site for the castle was selected, the ground plan was marked out to the proper scale, and the turf dug at the chosen spot. Stones were then raised to the height of six feet all round the building, in order to judge of the views from the lower windows. And all this being

done they found to their mortification that
sight was lost of a certain piece of river and
an old stone bridge which they had calculated
on getting into the perspective. Lord Blessington was not a man to allow obstacles of any
kind to stand between him and his wishes;
so the young architect received orders to
change the course of the river, that it might
be brought into view; then an ugly hill on the
other side was to be carted away, whilst a
big bare mountain likewise objectionable,
which might not readily lend itself to such
treatment, was to be planted with firs and
larch, for which purpose a hundred and fifty
thousand were removed from the nursery to
the spot.

'Are not these grand doings?' asks young
Mathews in writing to his mother.

The pleasant task of planning the fairy
palace did not wholly occupy the time of host
and guest, who diverted themselves with stag-
hunting, rabbit-shooting, sight-seeing, and play-
acting between whiles; when Mathews who
inherited his father's talents and was a capital

mimic, an excellent actor, and a rare story-
teller, appeared as the hero in ' Jeremy Diddler ' ;
Charles Gardiner my lord's illegitimate son,
playing Fainwould ; and the Earl representing
Sam. The country gentry were invited and
great fun followed. Concerning one of these
who probably had drunk overmuch of the best
claret in Ireland, Mathews tells a delightful
anecdote not to be omitted.

This individual was offered a bed and 'he
undressed himself in his dressing-room, put
out his candle and entered his bedroom. But
after groping round and round the room for
some time, he could not find any bed, and
there being no bell, he laid himself down on
the rug and slept till morning. On awakening
he discovered that there was a most beautiful
bed in the middle of the room.'

Now the fairy palace having been raised to
the height of six feet, the Earl discovered that
nothing more could be done until Lady Blessington had seen and approved of the plans ;
and he therefore proposed to carry the young
and docile architect with him to Naples where

she might be consulted and all further details carried out under her instructions. The lad's parents were asked to consent to this arrangement, and the elder Mathews wrote that he could not find language 'to convey the high sense I have of the honour and friendship you have conferred on me in the person of Charles, nor of the gratification I feel that you deem him worthy of the proposed distinction of residing with Lady Blessington and yourself during the winter;' whilst as for Mrs Mathews 'she was anxious to waive all selfish consideration in order to give him the whole advantage of your lordship's invaluable friendship, and regardless of aught else, to insure his welfare in your continued kind feelings towards him. With all thankfulness for so unexpected and great proof of it, she yields up Charles to your lordship's and Lady Blessington's entire direction ; well assured and satisfied that under such auspices and associations, he must acquire much, and improve in all things that can insure him present delight and lasting honour.'

Young Mathews was delighted at the

prospect of seeing Italy, the land of his dreams, he could scarcely believe his good fortune, and for days he walked on air. There was a quick return to London where hasty preparations were made. Then on the morning of the 21st of September 1823, he bade his parents good-bye ; eyes were wiped, and handkerchiefs were waved to him who seated beside his patron in a well-laden travelling carriage with four post horses, was driven at a smart rate from St James's Square.

A world of wonders opened up before the young man's sight, and he had ample time to examine whatever interested him, owing to his lordship's habits : for the Earl loved his ease and had no desire to hurry ; he was not a walker, and sight-seeing bored him ; he breakfasted in bed and there read his newspapers and books, rising late in the day, so that Mathews saw little of him save when travelling or at meal-times. Fortunately for the young man, Lord Blessington had another travelling companion in the person of Sir Charles Sutton, who bore Mathews company in his excursions abroad, and his visits to palaces, churches, and galleries.

Seven days after their departure from London they had crossed the Jura and reached Geneva, where to their astonishment they met Lady Blessington's sister Mrs John Home Purves with her children and governesses, and the Hon. Manners Sutton, when Lord Blessington pressed them to accompany him to Naples, an invitation which they were unable to accept. After two months' travelling they reached Milan, where Lord Blessington bought another carriage. As an instance of the tediousness which travellers endured in those days, it may be mentioned that in journeying from Genoa to Chiavari they fell in at about five o'clock in the afternoon with Lord Haywarden, who had started from Spezia at half-past four in the morning, and had only covered a distance of seven miles meantime. He advised them not to continue their journey, much rain had fallen, the roads were covered with water and almost impassable, and he had seen a carriage with ladies which had been for four hours stuck in the river, from which ten horses had been unable to drag them.

Lord Blessington would not of course listen to advice, and soon he came to part of a road crossed by a swollen stream, when he was obliged to hire twenty stalwart peasants to drag them through the water and push the carriages up a hill. Then they reached Borghetto and took refuge in a hut called by courtesy an inn. There was but one bedroom which was given up to my lord, two other beds being brought into the *salle-à-manger* for his companions. Rain poured in torrents all night, an incessant noise was kept up, and any stray pigs that were passing by graciously looked in on the young Englishmen.

As for the room occupied by the elegant and luxurious Lord Blessington 'it was the acme of misery, and yet with a comic side to it. A small truck bed with a little alcove at the further end, over which was the staircase whose creaking boards completely banished sleep: Lord Blessington in a large flannel night-cap, with a travelling shawl over his shoulders, sitting up in bed with his books and drawings strewed around him, his breakfast by his side, served in the silver accessories of his travelling kit; a poor little rickety table set out with all the profusion of costly plate and cut-glass bottles of the emptied dressing-case, with brocaded dressing-gowns on the broken-backed chairs, and imperials piled on imperials almost reaching the ceiling and actually filling the room. It was a splendid subject for a picture. I must do him the justice' writes Mathews 'to say he bore his situation manfully.'

It was impossible for them to quit this place until the floods which swamped the roads subsided, and meanwhile the rain fell black and steady. Now to while away the weary hours, my lord and his young friend covered the newly white-washed walls with grand cartoons; the Earl drawing a portrait of Napoleon on horseback surrounded by his generals, the architect picturing the great temple at Pæstum. They were eventually obliged to leave the carriages behind them,

and to travel across swollen torrents on horseback, whilst their luggage was carried in sedan
chairs.

And so after many strange adventures by flood
and field they reached their destination. 'What
words can adequately describe the paradise
to which I was introduced at Naples?' asks
Mathews. 'The Palazzo Belvedere, situated
about a mile and a half from the town on
the heights of Vomero, overlooking the city,
and the beautiful turquoise-coloured bay dotted
with latine sails, with Vesuvius on the left, the
island of Capri on the right, and the lovely coast
of Sorrento stretched out in front, presented
an enchanting scene. The house was the
perfection of an Italian palace, with its exquisite frescoes, marble arcades, and succession
of terraces one beneath the other, adorned with
hanging groves of orange trees and pomegranates, shaking their odours among festoons
of vines and luxuriant creepers, affording
agreeable shade from the noontide sun, made
brighter by the brilliant *parterres* of glowing
flowers, while refreshing fountains plashed in

every direction among statues and vases in-numerable. I was naturally entranced and commenced a new existence.

'Lady Blessington then in her youth, and certainly one of the most beautiful as well as one of the most fascinating women of her time, formed the centre figure in the little family group assembled within its precincts.

'Count D'Orsay was the next object of attraction, and I have no hesitation in assert-ing was the beau ideal of manly dignity and grace. He had not yet assumed the marked peculiarities of dress and deportment which the sophistications of London life subsequently developed. He was the model of all that could be conceived of noble demeanour and youthful candour; handsome beyond all question; accomplished to the last degree; highly educated, and of great literary acquire-ments; with a gaiety of heart and cheerful-ness of mind that spread happiness on all around. His conversation was brilliant and engaging as well as clever and instructive. He was moreover the best fencer, dancer, swimmer, runner, dresser; the best shot, the best horseman, the best draughtsman of his age. Possessed of every attribute that could render his society desirable, I am sure I do not go too far in pronouncing him the perfection of a youthful nobleman.

Then came Miss Power, Lady Blessington's youngest sister somewhat demure in aspect, of quiet and retiring manners, contrasting sweetly with the more dazzling qualities which sparkled around her. Lady Blessington has been described as a peach blossom, and Miss Power as a primrose by her side.

The great *salon* of the villa occupied its centre, and here in one corner was Lady Blessington's table covered with flowers, books and writing materials, in another corner Miss Power had her table, Count D'Orsay his in a third filled with artistic litter, whilst a fourth was given to Mathews where he might map out his plans and draw his designs. My lord had an adjoining sanctum all his own, in and out of which he strolled continually, asking questions, proposing some party of pleasure, or speaking of his occupations, the designs for his castle and the plot of the novel he was then engaged in writing. Regarding the former he told a friend ' I discovered that Lady Blessington did not like our plan, and so without arguing the topic I determined upon abandoning it. Knowing also how difficult if not impossible it is to do anything which everybody likes, I determined to make a residence out of my present cottage which everybody dislikes.' -

The fact that all idea of erecting the fairy palace was abandoned was concealed from the young architect, who continued to sketch the famous ruins, churches, and palaces in the neighbourhood. His hosts were anxious to keep under their roof a young man of so lively a spirit, so entertaining a manner, buoyant, clever, a maker of epigrams, a writer of *Vers de Société*, a surprising mimic, a clever sketcher, wonderful in his impromptus, an excellent actor, and withal full of tact, amiable, frank, and lovable.

Now he was getting up theatricals, in which Miss Power in a pair of white trousers, buff waistcoat, and blue frock-coat, with beard, moustaches and eyebrows made of cork, was introduced as a young Spanish gentleman : he himself was disguised 'as a nice old doctor bulky and powdered' with black net breeches, white silk stockings and large buckles ; whilst the Countess who made one of the amateurs was dressed as an old lady in an embroidered silk gown, a cap, and a quantity of curls in front, powdered. 'I never in my life saw anything so perfectly beautiful' writes the lad to his mother. 'I would have given a hundred pounds for you to have seen her. You never saw such a darling as she was altogether.'

Again he was providing his hosts and their guests with entertainment which he alone provided. In a marvellously short time he had picked up the Neapolitan dialect, manner and peculiarities, and with these in his possession he gave imitations of characters well known to the town. Amongst those the individual who recited 'Ariosto and Tasso to an entranced crowd. Then he imitated the mendicants, the street preachers, and musicians whose songs he sang to an accompaniment on the guitar, as after dinner he with his friends sat in the loggia overlooking the bay, the caressing warmth of a southern night in the air, the yellow moonlight full upon the bay.

Once when Miss Power was ill and had sixty leeches applied to her in three days, Mathews, in order to divert her, dressed himself as a doctor and visited her. After sitting down beside and talking to her for some time, he took the nurse aside to ask her some droll questions which the woman not recognising him answered in detail, and even consulted him on several subjects. Then D'Orsay very serious of mein took her out of the room to inquire what the doctor had said, and presently sent her in again to ask another question, but on her return no doctor was visible, only young Mathews who had put away his wig. She searched the room for the medical man and would not be convinced she had been hoaxed until the wig was replaced and the grave manner resumed, when her astonishment became the most laughable thing in the world.

This personation was such a success that next evening when Sir William Gell, Keppel Craven, Prince Lardaria and Count Lieven came to dinner, Mathews was asked to represent the doctor once more. So away he stole and presently sent down word to say that having visited Miss Power, he wished to pay his respects to her ladyship. Immediately after he was shown into the room when the guests who had no suspicion of his individuality, all rose. My lady played her part, asked questions concerning his patient, and spoke of the climate. He was next requested to sing the song he had made a few days before, when he complied by giving them 'One Hundred Years Ago.' Then he told them unintelligible ancedotes, made jokes, and took his leave undiscovered by the strangers.

When he re-entered in his own person, they began to tell him of the old bore who had just quitted them, and D'Orsay asked that Mathews might give his imitation of the doctor's song, which he sang over again precisely as before. The imitation was declared excellent by all except Prince Lardaria, who remarked it did not give him the idea of so old a man; much to his confusion when the truth was told him.

But even my lady was fated to be deceived by her lively guest, for next morning he arranged his hair, put on moustaches, changed his dress and manner, and arrived at breakfast as Count Lieven. Lady Blessington rose and made him an elegant courtesy when he burst out laughing much to her surprise, and the secret was out. But entering into his joke she insisted he should visit her sister, on which he was introduced to the bedroom of the invalid who was overcome with shame that the Count should have been allowed to enter.

Between work and play, many delightful months passed for Charles Mathews who writing to his mother in June 1824 says:—

'We are most happy in Belvedere, for during the hot months it is the only breathing place that can be found. The sea air is always fresh, and the terraces always cool, admitting of the most enchanting walks by the light of the moon : indeed nothing can equal these terraces, overlooking the bay, and perfumed with the exquisite fragrance of the flowers below.

'An Italian moonlight differs materially from ours in England from the total absence of all fog, or damp mists; not even the slightest dew is perceptible. Not a breath of air is stirring or a sound of any kind to be heard except the exquisite melody of our darling nightingales who from the groves above which we stand and in which we are enveloped, burst forth at short intervals with all that brilliancy and richness so often celebrated, but in such perfection so seldom heard. Belvedere at this hour is elevated into the very highest heaven of poetry. Every moonlight scene that ever was described, is here realised and surpassed. That glorious combination of sea, mountain, and island under the soothing gentle light of the church

Diana, is viewed with a feeling of reverent admiration that absolutely inspires the soul with an unearthly delight.

'The perfect clearness with which every object is visible is quite inconceivable. In the midst of the glistening reflection of the pale light on the glassy surface of the sea, is frequently seen the small white sail of the fishing-boat gliding in silence through the calm water, or the shining gondola enjoying the heavenly scene, training after it a long line of silvery brightness, and sometimes the subdued sounds of their distant music falling upon the ear. It is really enchanting, and each night with various effects of light, I enjoy it from the terrace which adjoins my bedroom when all the rest of the house are quietly asleep. Here I literally sit for hours in my morning-gown, without the least desire to sleep, watching with delighted eye the fireflies, their golden wings glistening as they chase each other from place to place, and sometimes quite illuminating by their numbers the deep purple shade of the garden.'

CHAPTER VI

WITHIN five weeks of the departure of Lady
Blessington from Genoa, Byron had started
for Greece. Bearing in mind his superstitious
feelings it may be considered strange that he
set sail on a Friday ; a day on which he had
a horror of transacting any business or of
beginning any enterprise.

Once when at Pisa he had set out to visit
a friend at her new residence, but before reaching the door he remembered the day was
Friday, on which he hurriedly turned back,
not wishing, as he said, to make his first visit

on that day; and later he had sent away a Genoese tailor who had dared to bring home a new coat on the same ominous day.

But now in taking so important a step in his life, either forgetful of the day in the midst of his excitement, or believing that it was immaterial on what day he began an undertaking which he felt assured would be fatal to him, he set sail for Greece on a Friday, embarking in an English brig the *Hercules* which he had chartered to convey himself and his suite consisting of Count Gamba, Captain Trelawney, Dr Bruno, and eight servants.

At sunrise of a clear July morning they left the port, but there being no wind they remained all day in sight of Genoa with her palaces and gardens looking down from her superb heights upon the sea. Night came with a weird moon looking ghastly upon a wild procession of ominous clouds scudding in fright apast her; the wind rose and woke the storm, a terror-struck sea dashed round them, and for a time the *Hercules* and her crew were in serious danger. Eventually the captain was enabled to gain the port once more, just as a blood-red dawn smeared the grey-green sky when Byron and his friends chilled, drenched, and overwrought, landed. He insisted on visiting his palace once more, and reached it as the triumphant light of the new-born day made the Casa beautiful to the eyes of one who thought to behold it no more: but the poet reached his home only to find it a desolate and an empty place holding nothing but melancholy memories: for early that morning Count Gamba had taken his daughter from a house whose every spot mocked her by its associations with happiness, and had driven with her, half-dazed and inert from grief, to Boglona. Throughout the day Byron looked thoughtful and depressed, remarked with a forced ironic laugh that such a bad beginning of his voyage was a favourable omen for its happy ending. Then by a quick transit of ideas he dwelt upon his past life and touched upon the uncertainty of the future, and turning to Count Gamba asked 'Where shall we be in a year?'

It looked, as the Count afterwards stated 'like a melancholy foreboding: for on the same day of the same month, in the next year, he was carried to the tomb of his ancestors.'

It took the greater part of a day to repair the damage done to the brig, and when evening came Byron set sail once more. The weather was now favourable and the poet endeavoured to cast aside his gloom. In August he reached the Ionian Isles. Whilst at Cephalonia he wrote to the Countess Guiccioli begging her to be as cheerful and tranquil as she could. 'Be assured' he says 'that there is nothing here that can excite anything but a wish to be with you again.'

Later still he tells her that the moment he can join her will be as welcome to him as any period of their recollection. From Cephalonia he set sail for Missolonghi where on the 22d of January 1824, he completed his thirty-sixth year, on which occasion he composed some verses which he thought were much better than he usually wrote; the second of which runs :—

' My days are in the yellow leaf ;
    The flowers and fruits of love are gone ;
    The worm, the canker, and the grief,
        Are mine alone.'

It was on the fifteenth of the following
month when harassed, disappointed by ingratitude and unsettled, he was seized by
convulsions so violent that two men were
obliged to hold him ; his agony being so
intense the while that he felt had they lasted
a moment longer he must have died. So
soon as he could speak he showed himself
free from all alarm, and coolly asked if this
attack was likely to prove fatal. ' Let me
know ' he said. ' Do not think I am afraid to
die—I am not.'

On the following morning he was weak
and pale, and as he complained of feeling
a weight in his head, leeches were applied
to his temples : on their removal it was
found difficult to prevent a flow of blood
and he fainted from exhaustion. As he was
lying in bed ' with his whole nervous system
completely shaken, the mutinous Suliotes,

covered with dirt and splendid attires, broke into his apartment, brandishing their costly arms and loudly demanding their wild rights. Lord Byron electrified by this unexpected act, seemed to recover from his sickness, and the more the Suliotes raged, the more his calm courage triumphed.' The scene was truly sublime! as Colonel Stanhope who was present states.

·This scene was but a supplement to 'the shooting and slashing in a domestic quiet way' that formed part of his housekeeping. He soon looked forward to the recovery of his health and the beginning of his campaign when he proposed to take the field at the head of his own brigade and the troops which the Government of Greece were to place under his orders. But he failed to recover so rapidly as he expected; for he frequently complained of vertigos that made him feel as if intoxicated, of nervous sensations, of nervousness and tremours, all of which he attributed to full habit.

Accordingly he lived on dry toast, vegetables

and cheese, drank only water, and continually measured himself round the waist and wrists when, if he thought himself getting stout he took strong doses of medicine; for in leaving Italy he had taken 'medicines enough for the supply of a thousand men for a year.' His friends strove to persuade him to return to Cephalonia where he might have a better chance of recovering his health than at Missolonghi where heavy rains had rendered the swamps impassable, and where a plague had broken out, so that obliged to remain indoors he had no exercise save drilling and single stick; but he refused to leave.

Becoming impatient of confinement, he rode out one day with Count Gamba, when they were overtaken by a heavy shower which drenched them. A couple of hours after the poet had returned home he was seized with shudderings and complained of fever. But next day he was again in the saddle, but once more was subjected to shudderings which caused him much pain. 'I do not care for death' he said 'but these agonies I cannot

bear.' His illness was pronounced to be
rheumatic fever and he kept his bed. He was
now unable to gain sleep or to take nourish-
ment, he suffered from his head and grew
weaker. He became afraid that he was losing
his memory to test which he repeated some
Latin verses with their English translation
which he had not striven to remember since
his school-days.

His doctors wished to reduce his inflammatory
symptoms by bleeding, but to this he offered
the strongest objection, quoting from an essay
recently published that less slaughter was
effected by the lance than by the lancet: and
stating that they might do what they pleased
with him, but bleed him they should not. If
his hour had come, he would die, whether he
lost or kept his blood. •

These persuasions were renewed next day,
they telling him that unless he changed his
resolution his disease might operate in such a
way as to deprive him for ever of reason: an
argument that had its effect, for partly annoyed
and partly persuaded, he cast at the doctor's

the fiercest glance of vexation, and throwing out his arm said in the angriest tone 'There, you are I see a damned set of butchers, take away as much blood as you like but have done with it.'

The blood was drawn but the result not being such as was expected the operation was twice repeated next day, as appearances of inflammation of the brain were hourly increasing. Count Gamba, and the poet's valet Fletcher, were in tears which they strove to conceal by hastening from the room. Captain Parry who had formed the expedition says that 'in all the attendants there was the officiousness of zeal: but owing to their ignorance of each other's language, their zeal only added to the confusion. This circumstance, and the want of common necessaries, made Lord Byron's apartment such a picture of distress and even anguish during the last two or three days of his life, as I never before beheld and wish never again to witness.'

The end came soon. Periods of delirium ensued, followed by recovery of consciousness. On being asked by Fletcher whether he should bring pen and paper to take down his words, Byron answered 'There is no time —it is now nearly over. Go to my sister tell her—go to Lady Byron you will see her and say—' then his voice became indistinct and he muttered.

'My lord' said the sorrowing Fletcher 'I have not understood a word your lordship has been saying.'

'Not understood me?' said Byron in bitter distress 'what a pity—then it is too late—all is over.'

'I hope not' answered the valet 'but the Lord's will be done.'

'Yes, not mine' the poet replied.

A strong antispasmodic potion was given him which produced sleep. When he woke he said 'Why was I not aware of this sooner? My hour is come, I do not care for death, but why did I not go home before I came here. There are things which make the world dear to me; for the rest I am content to die.'

Towards six in the evening he said 'Now

I shall go to sleep' and turning round he fell into a slumber from which he woke no more: his death happened on the 19th of April 1824.

One evening in the following month news was brought to the Palazzo Belvedere of Byron's death, news which coming suddenly upon its residents, filled them with awe and gloom. For that night and for days to come, their spirits were subdued, and their thoughts were turned in the same direction. Each recalled some trait of the poet's; some characteristic speech; they dwelt upon his farewell visit to them, and valued more than before the trifling gifts he had given them. Lady Blessington read over the notes she had made of his conversations, and as she did it seemed as if his voice had spoken the words.

'Alas, alas' she writes 'his presentiment of dying in Greece has been but too well fulfilled — and I used to banter him on this superstitious presentiment. Poor Byron, long, long will you be remembered by us with feelings of deep regret.'

After a residence of nearly three years in Naples the Blessingtons resolved to leave that city of delight. The length of her stay and her attachment to the people made it painful for the Countess to depart. During the last week of her sojourn her *salon* was nightly crowded by those who were anxious to spend as much time as possible in her company; whilst a vast number of gifts were given her by way of remembrances.

She could not bring herself to think she was quitting Naples for ever, and she strove to keep her spirits up by a hope of revisiting a place so full of happy memories; but when the time came for saying farewell she cried bitterly and freely, her friends being not less moved.

Leaving Naples they hurried through Rome, made a short stay at Florence, and reached Genoa in December 1826. Lord Blessington had now determined to return to England, but eventually he changed his mind, and they retracing their steps, spent about six months in Pisa; and in the spring of 1827 arrived in Florence then rich in the wealth of its flowers.

At first they stayed at the hotel Schneiderff, but the perpetual bustle and the continual odour of cooking fatigued my lady who sought for a quieter residence and eventually took the Casa Pecori, which had once belonged to Elise Bacciocchi Duchess of Tuscany. The villa was charmingly situated, its principal windows opening on a terrace bordered by orange trees and overlooking the Arno.

Once established here the Blessingtons threw open their doors and received the most distinguished men of the day. Amongst these were two who particularly interested their hostess: one being Monsieur de Lamartine the French poet, statesman and traveller; the other a man of rare genius, Walter Savage Landor.

Lady Blessington's impressions of Lamartine are amusing to read: according to her he had 'a *presence d'esprit* not often to be met with in the generality of poets; and a perfect freedom from any of the affectations of

manner attributed to that *genus irritabile.'*
But more remains behind : for we learn he was
handsome, distinguished 'and dresses so perfectly like a gentleman that one would never
suspect him to be a poet. No shirt-collars
turned over an apology for a cravat, no long
curls falling on the collar of the coat, no
assumption of any foppishness of any kind ;
but just the sort of man that seen in any
society would be pronounced *bien comme il
faut.'* Lord Blessington had been previously
acquainted with Landor and on coming to
Florence the Earl soon sought out the author
whom he subsequently introduced to Lady
Blessington. Concerning him she had heard
much from acquaintances and had looked
forward to their meeting with some anxiety.

Landor who was at this time in his fifty-
first year, was a Warwickshire squire, a learned
scholar, a man of original mind, and the
author of *Imaginary Conversations.* Even
whilst a Rugby boy he became famous for
his skill in making Latin verses, and later
when he entered Trinity College Oxford, he

was not less renowned for his ability to make
Greek verse. Though these were, according
to his own belief, the best in the university,
it was strongly characteristic of him that here,
as at Rugby, he refused to compete for the
prizes.

The waywardness of his temper, his unbend-
ing will, his defiance of authority and self-
reliance, had shown themselves from an early
age. When as a sturdy lad he went a-fishing
with a cast net and met with a farmer who
interfered with this pastime, Landor replied
by flinging the net over him and holding him
captive ; when Dr James headmaster of Rugby
selected for approbation some verses which
Landor did not consider his best, he gratified
his indignation by writing on the fair copy
made of them, some insulting remarks, and this
action being repeated, Dr James asked that
the boy might be removed to avoid the
necessity of expulsion.

Whilst at Oxford which he entered in 1793,
he gave offence by going into the hall with
his hair unpowdered by way of illustrating

his tendencies to republicanism ; he wrote an ode to Washington, and was not displeased to be termed 'a mad Jacobine.' Later followed a freak which brought him into trouble. One evening whilst entertaining friends at a wine party he saw that a Tory undergraduate who occupied rooms opposite, was similarly engaged, though the guests of the latter according to Landor 'consisted of servitors and other raffs of every description.' Taunts and jeers were exchanged by both parties until the Tories closed their window shutters, on which Landor treated them to a few shots. Though no harm was done much noise was made. Landor refused all explanations and was as a consequence rusticated for a year.

This widened a misunderstanding which had already existed between himself and his father, a stormy scene followed their meeting, when Landor left his father's house as he declared and believed for ever, and going up to London published a volume of English and Latin poems.

Eventually peace was made between father

and son; when the former offered the latter
four hundred a year if he would study law; but
proposed to give him a hundred and fifty a year
with permission to live at home whenever he
pleased, if he refused to take up a profession.
Walter who all his life hated restraint, preferred
liberty and the smaller sum, and taking himself into Wales remained there some three
years. His father died in 1805, when Walter
being the eldest son had money and to spare.
Three years after this date, when the Spaniards
rose against the French, Landor joined the
Spanish army in whose expeditions he took
part.

When he was six-and-thirty and at a period
when he was writing 'Count Julian' he one
night entered a ballroom at Bath, and seeing a
pretty girl asked her name. He was told it
was Julia Thuillier, on which he exclaimed 'By
Heaven that's the nicest girl in the room, and
I'll marry her.' A few days later he writes to
his friend Southey 'It is curious that the evening of my beginning to transcribe the tragedy,
I fell in love. I have found a girl without a

sixpence, and with very few accomplishments. She is pretty, graceful, and good-tempered— three things indispensable to my happiness. Adieu and congratulate me.' Later he spoke to his mother of his intended bride as a girl 'who had no pretensions of any kind, and her want of fortune was the very thing which determined me to marry her.' The marriage took place in haste and was repented at leisure. Mrs Landor was a simple insignificant little woman who bore children, delighted in house-keep, and exhibited a nagging disposition to her husband. 'God forbid,' Landor said on one occasion 'that I should do otherwise than declare that she always *was* agreeable — to everyone but *me.*'

A couple of years after his marriage he resolved to live in France, a plan to which his wife strongly objected. In what part of that country he would end his days he had not yet decided, 'but there I shall end them' he writes to a friend 'and God grant that I may end them speedily, so as to leave as little sorrow as possible to my friends.' No day passed that

his wife did not urge her disinclination to live
abroad, he subdued his temper 'the worst
beyond comparison that man was ever cursed
with' as he acknowledges. One evening whilst
they were staying at Jersey her irritating ob-
jections were renewed; she nagged for an hour
and a half without a syllable of reply from him
'but every kind and tender sentiment was
rooted up from my heart for ever' he writes.
At last exasperated she who was sixteen years
his junior, reproached herself with 'marrying
such an old man.'

Landor could stand this no longer and hurried
away to his room, heart sick and weary, and
remained tossing about, broad awake for hours.
He rose at four o'clock, walked to the other
side of the island and embarked alone on an
oyster boat bound for France, resolved never to
see her more.

'I have neither wife nor family, nor house nor
home, nor pursuit, nor occupation' he writes.
'Every man alive will blame me; many will
calumniate me; and all will cherish and rejoice
in the calumny. All that were not unjust to me

before will be made unjust to me by her. A thousand times have I implored her not to drive me to destruction : to be contented if I acknowledged myself in the wrong : to permit me to be at once of her opinion, and not to think a conversation incomplete without a quarrel. The usual reply was, " A pleasant sort of thing truly, that you are never to be contradicted." As if it were extraordinary and strange that one should wish to avoid it. She never was aware that more can be said in one minute than can be forgotten in a lifetime.'

Poor Landor, no wonder he wrote years later ' Death itself to the reflecting mind is less serious than marriage.'

A reconciliation was in due time effected when his sister-in-law wrote to acquaint him of his wife's extreme grief, with the fact that she was seriously ill, and of her desire to join him. This banished from his generous mind all traces of resentment and he ' wrote instantly to comfort and console her.' ' My own fear is ' he adds ' that I shall never be able to keep my promise in its full extent, to forgive humiliating and insulting language. Certainly I shall never be so happy as I was before : that is beyond all question.'

They settled in town for some time and then went to Italy living for three years at Como where his first child was born. An insult to the authorities contained in a Latin poem was the cause of his being ordered to leave the place, when he went on to Pisa where he remained some three years before settling in a suite of rooms in the Palazzo Medice in Florence in 1821. Here he became a notable figure re-marked by all for his eccentricities, beloved by many for his characteristics. His courtesy to women was only equalled by his love of children ; his generosity was ever excessive; his affection for animals led him to treat them as human beings ; and flowers were to him as living things. But his temper forever banished peace.

Scarcely had he been settled in Florence when he conceived himself to have been treated 'with marked indignation' by the Secretary of the English Legation, so that he was obliged to ask that individual 'in what part of England or

France they might become better acquainted
in a few minutes.' The offending individual
was a poor spirited wretch who had no taste for
a duel; but it appeared there was no end to the
insults he was capable of offering; for he posi-
tively presumed to whistle in the streets whilst
passing Mrs Landor. 'This' her husband thinks
'has affected her health, and I am afraid may
oblige me to put him to death before we can
reach England. Is it not scandalous that our
ministry should employ such men? I have a
presentiment that you will hear something of me
which you would rather not hear, but my name
shall be respected as long as it is remembered.'
Blood was spared over this affair, but not ink :
for Landor wrote a letter to the Foreign Minister
in Downing Street telling him that some curious
facts were in his possession 'concerning more
than one of the wretches he has employed
abroad.'

Later than this he accused his landlord the
Marquis de Medici of having enticed away
his coachman. Next day whilst Landor, his
wife, and some friends were sitting in the

drawing-room the offended Marquis came strut-
ting in with his hat on: but he had not advanced three steps from the door when Landor
walked quickly up to him, knocked his hat
off and then taking him by the arm conducted
the astonished Marquis to the door.

As to his personal appearance Landor was
wholly indifferent. It was his custom to
wear his clothes until they could scarcely
hang together; and years before when he
used to visit his sisters, who were offended by
his carelessness in this respect, they would
leave new garments by his bedside which he
would put on in the morning without discovering the change.

The wondering Italians on seeing him used
to say all the English were mad, but this
one more than the rest.

Many English visitors to Florence made
the acquaintance and friendship of this original
man, but with none of them did he become
so intimate as with the Blessingtons. The
strong magnetic charm which few who approached Lady Blessington failed to experi-

ence, was felt from the first by Landor whom it swayed to the end. On her part she was struck by the dignity and urbanity of his manner, his fearless courage in the expression of his opinions, his contempt for what he considered unworthy, the simplicity of his mode of life from which self-gratification was rigidly excluded, his profuse generosity and his almost womanly tenderness.

She had been led to think him eccentric and violent, but she confesses that the only singularity she can find in him is 'his more than ordinary politeness towards women— a singularity that I heartily wish was one no longer.' Then his fine intellectual head with its broad prominent forehead, the eyes quick and expressive, and the mouth full of benevolence, pleased her greatly.

Finding Lady Blessington sympathetic and charming, a brilliant conversationalist and what was more a willing listener, Walter Savage Landor visited her every evening from eight to eleven, as he narrates, during his stay in Florence, and when he moved to

Fiesole a distance of three miles, he spent two evenings a week in her delightful company.

And what conversations they had, for on any and on every subject he was ready and willing to vent decided opinions in vigorous English, an idea of which may be gained from the contents of his letters. For instance she must not praise him for his admiration of Wordsworth and Southey. That was only a proof that he was not born to be a poet. He was not a good hater; he only hated pain and trouble. He thought he could have hated Bonaparte if he had been a gentleman, but he was so thorough a blackguard, thief, and swindler, that wherever he appeared contempt held the shield before hatred. Robert Stewart, Viscount Castlereagh, afterwards second Marquis of Londonderry, was almost as mischievous and was popularly a gentleman, but being an ignorant and a weak creature he escaped from hatred without a bruise. And wasn't it remarkable how very few people of the name of Stewart had ever been good for anything. He had known a dozen or two, and the best of them was Dan Stewart a poacher at Oxford whom he had introduced into his 'Penn and Peterborow.'

It was amongst the few felicities of his life that he had never been attached to a party or been a party man. He had always excused himself from dinners that he might not meet one. The English must be the most quiet and orderly people in the universe, not to rush into the houses of the rapacious demagogues, and tie them by the necks in couples and throw them *tutti quanti* into the Thames.

As for himself, he never cared one farthing what people thought about him, and had always avoided the intercourse and notice of the world. He would readily stand up to be measured by those who were high enough to measure him— men such as Coleridge, Southey, and Wordsworth. They had done it, and as their measurement agreed he was bound to believe it correct, although his own fingers would have made him an inch lower. A little while ago he was praised only by such as these. Taylor and Leigh Hunt, both admirable poets, had since measured him beyond his expectations. He did not believe such kind things would be said of him for at least a century to come. Perhaps soon, even fashionable persons would pronounce his name without an apology, and he might be patted on the head by dandies with all the gloss upon their coats, and with unfrayed straps to their trousers. Who knew but that he might be encouraged at last to write as they instructed him, and might attract all the gay people of the parks and parliament by his puff-paste and powder-sugar surface.

Then it occurred to him that authors were beginning to think it an honest thing to pay their debts, and that they are debtors to all by whose labour and charges, the fields of literature have been cleared and sown. Few writers have said all the good they thought and said of others, and fewer have concealed the ill. They praise their friends, because their friends, it may be hoped, will praise them—or get them praised. As these propensities seemed inseparable from the literary character, he had always kept aloof from authors where he could. Southey stood erect and stood alone. Landor loved him no less for his integrity than for his genius.

Then he had been reading Beckford's travels and his romance *Vatheck*. The last pleased him less than it did forty years before, and yet the *Arabian Nights* had lost none of their charm for him. All the learned and wiseacres in England had cried out against the wonderful work upon its first appearance; Gray amongst the rest. Yet Landor doubted whether any man, except Shakespeare, had afforded so much delight if we open our hearts to receive it. The author of the *Arabian Nights* was the greatest benefactor the East ever had, not excepting Mahomet. How many hours of pure happiness had he bestowed on twenty-six millions of hearers. All the springs of the desert have less refreshed the Arabs than those delightful tales, and they cast their gems and genii over our benighted and foggy regions.

Regarding dogs, somebody had told him the

illustrious Goethe hated dogs. God forgive him if he did. He never could believe it of him. Dogs were half poets ; they were dreamers. Did any other animals dream ? For his own part he loved them heartily : they were grateful, they were brave, they were communicative, and they never played cards.

Then as to his children whom he worshipped. He could scarcely bring his eldest son Arnold to construe Greek with him, and what was worse he was not always disposed to fence. Landor foresaw the boy would be a worse dancer if possible than his father. In vain he told him what was true, that he had suffered more from his bad dancing than from all the other misfortunes and miseries of his life put together. Not dancing well he had never danced at all.

More than any words of friends or biographers, a letter written by himself throws a vivid light upon the original character of this man. Lady Blessington years later expressed a wish that he could be persuaded to write his memoirs. 'What a treasure would they prove to posterity' she says 'tracing the working of such a mind as yours, a mind that has never submitted to the ignoble fetters that a corrupt and artificial society would impose, could not fail to be highly interesting as well as useful, by giving courage to the timid and strength to the weak, and teaching them to rely on their intellectual resources, instead of leaning on that feeble reed the world, which can wound but not support those who rely on it.'

To which Landor made prompt answer—

'DEAR LADY BLESSINGTON,—It has quite escaped my memory whether I made any reply or remark on your flattering observation, that my life, written by myself, would interest the literary world and others. However, as you have repeated it, I will say a few words on the subject. I have always been cautious and solicitous to avoid the notice of the publick ; I mean individually and personally. Whatever I can write or do for their good is much at their service, and I do not disdain to amuse them, altho' I would not take any trouble about it. As for their curiosity in regard to

myself, it must remain ungratified. So little
did I court the notice of people even when
young, that I gave my Latin poems, etc., to the
printer on one only condition, namely, that he
should not even advertise them in the papers.
I never accepted an invitation to dinner in
London, excepting at your house and Sir
Charles Morgan's, *once.* He had taken a good
deal of trouble to bring thro' Parliament an
Inclosure Act of mine, in which, by means of
Sir Charles Mordaunt, Dugdale, himself, Lord
Manvers and Lord Walsingham, and I must
not forget Lord Oxford, I defeated the Duke
of Beaufort and his family, but encountered so
much opposition that altho' I had saved a
thousand pounds for my purpose, hardly one
shilling was left, and my four thousand acres
were and are still unenclosed. My own life-
holders opposed me, for there were but three
freeholders in the parish, and very small ones.
My own land was calculated at about eight
thousand acres; half enclosed, half not. I
always hated society and despised opinion.
Added to which, I must of necessity be a liar

in writing my life, since to conceal a truth or give a partial evidence is to lie. ✗ I spent thirteen winters of my early life in Bath, which at that time was frequented by the very best society. I was courted in spite of my bad temper, my unconciliating manners (to speak gently of them) and my republican opinions, I once even inspired love. There is no vanity in saying it. An old man or an old woman may say, pointing at the fireplace, " These ashes were once wood." But there are two things in this world utterly unpardonable—to say and to forget by whom we have been beloved. My rocks of Meillerie rise, but it is only in solitude that I will ever gaze upon them. I have nothing to do with people, nor people with me. A phrenologist once told me that he observed the mark of veneration on my head. I told him in return that I could give him a proof of it. I would hold the stirrup for Kosciusko, the brandy-bottle for Hofer, the standish for Southey, and I declare to you upon oath that I firmly believe myself superior to any duke, prince, king, emperor, or pope existing, as the best of these fellows is superior to the most sluggish and mangy turnspit in his dominions ; and I swear to you that I never will be, if I can help it, where any such folks are ✗ Why should I tell my countrymen these things ? Why should I make the worst-tempered nation in the world more sullen and morose than ever ? I love good manners, and therefore keep out of their way, avoiding all possibility of offence. I have been reading Sir Egerton Brydges' Autobiography. In one of the pages I wrote down this remark : Poor man ! He seems to be writing in the month of January in the city of London, the wind north-east, with his skin off. I would not live in London the six winter months for a thousand pounds a week. No, not even with the privilege of hanging a Tory on every lamp-arm to the right, and a Whig on every one to the left the whole extent of Piccadilly. This goes sadly against my patriotism. Do not tell any of the Radicals that I am grown so indifferent to the interests of our country. It appears that you have a change of ministry. I hope the Tories will leave Mr

Seymour his situation here as minister. He is the first in Tuscany that ever did his duty. How different from the idle profligate fiddler you remember here, and the insolent adventurer Dawkins. This ragamuffin, now minister in Greece, has lately been well described in the only work upon that country of any great use or merit, by Tiersch. Abundant proofs are given of his negligence and stupidity. Who would imagine that he had profited so little by living in such intimate familiarity with all the swindlers, spies, and jockeys in Tuscany? However, he is much improved, I hear. If he has not clean hands, he has clean gloves. I have reason to believe that King Otho has been informed of his character and of his subservience to the arbitrary acts of Capo D'Istra.'

CHAPTER VII

BEFORE the summer closed Lord Blessington
invited Landor to accompany him in his yacht
to Naples on an excursion which he was sure
would give pleasure to both. To this suggestion Landor readily agreed, for he had never
seen Naples and as he wrote to his sister he
'never could see it to such advantage as in the
company of a most delightful well-informed
man.' Lady Blessington remained in Florence
whilst the friends made their voyage.

Landor was delighted with all he saw. Those who had not seen the Bay of Naples could form no idea of its beauty from anything they had beheld elsewhere. La Cava was of all places one of the most beautiful. 'It lies in the way to Pæstum. The ruins of the temples here, if ruins they can be called, are magnificent : but Grecian architecture does not turn into ruin so grandly as Gothic. York Cathedral a thousand years hence, when the Americans have conquered and devastated the country, will be more striking.'

His pleasant trip was suddenly interrupted. At the time of his leaving Florence his boy Arnold, just recovered from a fever, had been pronounced quite convalescent, and had given his Babbo, as he styled his father, leave of absence for twenty-five days. On reaching Naples Landor failed to find a letter from home awaiting him. 'I was almost mad' he wrote to his sister 'for I fancied his illness had returned. I hesitated between drowning myself and going post back. At last I took a place (the only one ; for one only is allowed

with the postman in what is called the dili-
gence). Meanwhile Lord Blessington told me
he would instantly set sail if I wished it, and
that I could go quicker by sea. I did so;
and we arrived in four days at Leghorn.

'Here he gave me a note enclosed in a letter
to him, informing me that Julia had been in
danger of her life, but was now better. · I
found her quite unable to speak coherently;
and unhappily she was in the country. Nevertheless the physician, who sometimes passed
the whole day with her, and once slept at the
house, never omitted for forty-three days to
visit her twice a day, and now by his great
care she has reached Florence. I brought her
part of the way by means of oxen, on the
sledge, and upon two mattresses. To-day the
physician will attend her for the last
time.'

Mrs Landor had caught a malignant fever
which the youngest child had likewise taken,
a fever that might have spread to the other
children had not Lady Blessington driven to
where they were then staying in the country

and brought them away with her to her own residence.

After spending some eight months in Florence, the Blessingtons resolved to leave. Their departure was a sad blow to Landor, who could remember no pleasanter time of his life in Italy than the summer evenings passed with them in the Casa: for, as he wrote to his mother 'he had never talked with a woman more elegant or better-informed, more generous or high-minded' than Lady Blessington. So long as he remained in the city he never passed the house they had occupied without feelings of regret. 'It grieves me' he writes to Lady Blessington 'when I look up to the terrace; yet I never fail to look up at it when I am anywhere in sight, as if grief were as attractive as pleasure.' And then began his racy and delightful letters to her, his correspondence lasting till her death. Yet as a correspondent he seems to have entertained but a poor opinion of himself. 'Now all your letters are of value' he says to her 'and all mine stupid. I can write a scene in a tragedy with greater ease than a letter. I never know what to write about. And what not to say is a thousand times more difficult than what to say. But you always supply me with materials, and furnish me with a Grecian lamp to hang over them.'

This is a charming compliment, but not the most charming which he paid her as a correspondent : for he tells her on another occasion that he never entertains so high an opinion of his imagination as when reading her letters. 'They always make me fancy I hear and almost see you' he writes. Nor was Landor the only man of genius who especially valued this gift of hers. Years later Barry Cornwall writing to her says 'Your little letters always find me grateful to them. They (little paper angels as they are) put devils of all kinds from blue down to black to speedy flight.' And again this poet tells her 'Your little notes come into my Cimmerian cell like starlits shot from a brighter region—pretty and pleasant disturbers of the darkness about me. I imprison them (my Ariels) in a drawer, with conveyances and wills etc., and such sublunary things, which seem very proud of their society. Yet if your notes to me be skiey visitors, what must this *my* note be to *you*? It must I fear, be an evil genius.'

Her personality, atmosphere, or magnetism, that undefined potency which comes as a natural dower, without which it is impossible to impress with love or hatred; that subtle power which was found fascinating in her intercourse, was conveyed in her letters, and communicated its spell to their readers.

From Florence the Blessingtons proceeded to Rome which they reached in November 1827. The palace which had been engaged for them at a rental of forty pounds a month by no means commended itself to the Countess, and she immediately began a search for a residence more suitable to her desires. After a time this was found in the Palazzo Negroni where she engaged the two principal floors at the rate of a hundred guineas a month, for six months certain.

This being done she hired furniture at twenty-pounds a month, and produced from her own stores, eider-down pillows, curtains, and table covers with the aid of which she filled and brightened the three great *salons* the family were to occupy.

Then began anew that brilliant round of social life such as they had known in Naples and Florence. Scarce a day passed that they were not entertaining or being entertained. Such names as Count Funchal the Portuguese ambassador, Hallam the historian, Lord Howick, the Duc de Laval Montmorenci the French ambassador; the Princess de Montfort, Lord King, the Marchesa Conzani, the Marchesa Camarata, the Duc and Duchesse de Brucciano, flash through the pages of her diary as amongst those whom she received.

One night when Lady Blessington attended a bal masqué given by the Duchesse de Brucciano, she was struck by a figure moving amongst a thousand others in gorgeous coloured costumes, which figure, a female mask, presently addressed her, making witty and piquant remarks, and then turning away was lost in the brilliant maze around, leaving the Countess in wonder as to whom it was. But again the female mask appeared, and once more entering into conversation, announced that she was Hortense Bonaparte daughter of Josephine, and ex-queen of Holland, now styled the Duchesse de St Leu.

Before the night ended came another surprise. A mask in a blue domino had several times accosted her and kept up a lively conversation. Before they finally parted he confessed himself to be Jerome Bonaparte, brother of Napoleon, and ex-king of Westphalia, then known as the Prince de Montfort.

Lady Blessington willingly availed herself of an invitation extended to her by the ex-queen of Holland, who like everyone else soon felt the charm of her manner, and becoming friendly showed her the household gods she held dear ; amongst them some fine portraits of Napoleon and Josephine, her bed furniture and toilette service of gilt plate, and her jewels including a necklace of priceless diamonds presented by the city of Paris to Josephine, and others given to herself by the state of Holland. Nay, so pleased

was the ex-queen with her visitor, that she gave
her a turquoise and diamond ring which Josephine had worn for many years, and that her
daughter highly valued.

Then one day as Lady Blessington and her
party were walking in the gardens of the
Vigna Palatina, they were surprised by the
arrival of the Prince and Princess de Montfort with Madame Letitia Bonaparte, mother
of the great Napoleon, who was attended by
her chaplain, her *dame de compagnie*, and other
members of her suite. Having heard that
Madame Mère, as this mother of kings was
generally called, disliked meeting strangers,
the Blessington party retired to a distant
part of the garden; but the Prince having
recognised their carriage in the courtyard, sent
a message requesting that they would join him.

On obeying they were presented to his
mother and his wife. Madame Mère's tall
slight figure though bowed by age, preserved
its natural dignity and grace; her face, pale
and pensive was lighted by dark penetrat-
ing eyes; her snowy hair was parted above

a high forehead furrowed by care. Dressed in a robe of dark grey silk, 'a superb Cashmere shawl that looked like a tribute from some barbaric sovereign, fell gracefully over her shoulders,' her bonnet was worn over a lace cap.

In a low and tremulous voice she greeted those presented to her, and her eyes grew dim when she spoke of her great son whom she hoped 'soon to join in that better world where no tears where shed.' She added 'I thought I should have done so long ago, but God sees what is best for us.'

A faded figure, remarkable as the mother of the greatest man the modern world had produced, and pitiable as the survivor of his colossal wreckage, she walked in the noontide sun around the garden which Roman emperors had trod, weary of a life which had known such startling vicissitudes. Before driving away she said 'kind and flattering things' to Lady Blessington whom she invited to visit her, and then kissed her forehead in farewell.

A scarcely less interesting personage whom Lady Blessington met at this time was the Countess Guiccioli, now a prominent personage in Roman society. It has already been stated that whilst staying at Genoa, Lady Blessington had never seen Madame Guiccioli, though Byron had frequently mentioned her, and though her brother Count Gamba had been frequently entertained by the Blessingtons.

It was however at a *fête* given by the Duc de Laval Montmorenci that Lady Blessington first met the Contessa in whom she was much interested. With regular features, a delicately fair complexion, white teeth, beautiful red gold hair, a finely-moulded bust and well-shaped arms, she had every claim to be considered handsome; but there was an absence of any striking characteristic, of any exalted beauty which might naturally have been expected in one who had won the ardent love of a man like Byron, and stranger still who had kept it till his death.

At this time her husband was still amongst the living and she was depending upon the income he was compelled to allow her: for contrary to all expection save perhaps her own, her name was not mentioned in Byron's will. That he had at one time intended to leave her a considerable sum, there could be no doubt.

One day when he called on Lady Blessington he stated that he had been occupied all the morning in making his will, and that he had left the Countess Guiccioli ten thousand pounds, and would have made it twenty-five thousand but that she suspecting his intentions had urged him not to leave her any legacy. So fearful was she, he said, of the possibility of having interested motives attributed to her, that he was certain she would prefer to suffer poverty rather than to incur such suspicions; this being only one of the innumerable instances of her delicacy and disinterestedness, of which he had repeated proofs.

Lady Blessington suggested that if he left the Countess the sum he had originally intended, it would be a flattering proof of his affection for her; and that she would always have the power of refusing a part or the whole of the legacy if she wished ; to which he seemed to agree.

He also told his banker Mr Barry that he

intended to leave in his hands a will in which was a bequest of ten thousand pounds to Madame Guiccioli: and when leaving Greece the. poet instructed the banker to advance her money. This she would never consent to receive. When news came of Byron's death, Barry took it for granted that the will would be found amongst the sealed papers left with him by the poet, but no such document was discovered ; on which he immediately wrote to the Countess asking if she knew anything concerning it, mentioning at the same time what Byron had said regarding the legacy.

To this she replied that he had frequently spoken of the subject, but as it was painful to her she had always turned the.conversation and expressed a wish that no mention of her name would be found ; for her income was already sufficient for her wants 'and the world might put a wrong construction on her attachment, should it appear that her fortunes were in any degree bettered by it.' The Countess therefore, from a pecuniary point, in no ways benefited by Byron's attachment.

And now came an incident in the domestic life of the Blessingtons which was destined to have unhappy results for those it most concerned. It will be remembered that in April 1823 whilst they were at Genoa, news was brought to the Earl that his only legitimate son had died on the 26th of the previous month. The loss of his heir was a serious grief to Lord Blessington, especially as there seemed no probability of his being replaced, and the idea therefore occurred to the peer to make one of his daughters his heiress and marry her to his friend Alfred D'Orsay.

Which of the girls was destined to become the Countess D'Orsay he did not at first decide : both were at this time mere children ; the one, Emily Rosalie Hamilton born before her mother's marriage with Lord Blessington, but known as Lady Mary Gardiner being then in her twelfth year ; whilst the other his legitimate daughter Lady Harriet Anne Jane Frances Gardiner was twelve months younger. It was not of course intended that the marriage should take place for some time : both girls were then living in Dublin under the

care of their paternal aunt Lady Harriet
Gardiner, who resided with her brother-in-law
the Bishop of Ossory.

Accordingly on the 2d of June 1823 Lord
Blessington whilst at Genoa made a codicil to
his will in which he stated that having had
the misfortune to lose his beloved son 'and
having entered into engagements with Alfred
Comte D'Orsay, that an alliance should take
place between him and my daughter, which
engagement has been sanctioned by Albert
Comte D'Orsay, General etc. in the service
of France, this is to declare and publish my
desire to leave to the said Alfred D'Orsay
my estates in the city and county of Dublin
. . . for his and her use, whether it be
Mary (baptised Emily) Rosalie Hamilton, or
Harriet Anne Jane Frances, and to their heirs-
male, the said Alfred and said Mary or Harriet,
for ever in default of issue male, to follow the
provisions of the will and testament.'

Some two months later, on the 31st of August,
Lord Blessington made a last will and testament
to the same effect, the choice of his daughters

being still left open to the selection of the bridegroom, who had never seen either, and could
not but be indifferent to both.

To one of Count D'Orsay's nationality there
was nothing contrary to custom in the fact of
a girl he had never seen, being selected for and
accepted by him as his wife. As was usual in
such cases the matter had been arranged
between the fathers of the prospective bride
and bridegroom, and it merely remained for him
to agree to their wishes: an agreement which
was doubtless the more readily given in view
of the immense fortune which was to fall to him.

That Lord Blessington had selected D'Orsay
to become his son-in-law, can be explained only
on the ground of the high estimate in which he
held the Count's character and abilities and the
affection which the Earl entertained for him.
It was true that when the codicil containing
such a proposal was drawn up, D'Orsay had
been a member of their party merely for a few
months; but the four years which had elapsed
between this suggestion and the solemnisation
of the marriage, whilst giving Lord Blessing-

ton ample opportunity to see more of the Count, had not caused him to alter his mind meanwhile.

Had Lady Blessington from any motive, desired to prevent this marriage, there can be little doubt that her influence, which was supreme with her husband, could have effected her wishes: but the probability was that like the Earl, she considered that D'Orsay—a man of ancient lineage, possessing varied and brilliant talents and remarkable for his personal gifts —would in all ways prove a desirable member of their family.

It was eventually decided that the Earl's legitimate daughter, the Lady Harriet, was to become Count D'Orsay's wife, and she was therefore sent for, and arrived at Florence whilst the family were residing there.

Lady Harriet was at this time under seventeen. Slight and pale, silent and reserved, she seemed even younger than her age. She had never known her mother, had seen but little of her father, had no acquaintance with the world, was unused to strangers, and gave no indication

of the self-reliance and determination she afterwards showed. With searching, timid eyes she
looked at the polite foreigner to whom in future
she was to belong ; she, having no will to
sanction or to refuse the arrangement made for
her ; no thought but to obey. On his part
Count D'Orsay was not inspired with love by
this school-girl who seemed incapable of appreciating his best-turned compliments, and indifferent to the graces which had won him high
reputation in a hundred drawing-rooms.

It was originally the intention of Lord
Blessington that the marriage should take place
in Florence, but hindrance to this arrangement was given by the English Ambassador
in that city, John Lord Burghersh, afterwards
eleventh Earl of Westmoreland, who intimated
to the French Ambassador the Duke de Laval
Montmorenci that the ceremony according to
the rights of the English Church must precede
that of the Catholic Church. Moreover on some
personal remonstrance being made by Lady
Blessington he behaved with rudeness to her
and to her step-daughter ; an act which drew

from Walter Savage Landor the following wrathful letter :—

'DEAR LADY BLESSINGTON,—If I could hear of any wrong or any rudeness offered to you without at least as much resentment as you yourself would feel upon it, I should be unworthy not only of the friendship with which you honour me, but of one moment's thought or notice. Lord B. told me what had occurred yesterday. I believe I may have said on other occasions that nothing could surprise me, of folly or indecorum in Lord Burghersh. I must retract my words : the only ones he will ever make me retract. That a man educated among the sons of gentlemen could be guilty of such incivility to two ladies, to say nothing of condition, nothing of person, nothing of acquaintance and past courtesies, is inconceivable, even to the most observant of his behaviour throughout the whole period of his public life. From what I have heard and known during a residence of six years at Florence, I am convinced that all the ministers of all the other Courts in Europe (I may throw in those of Asia and Africa) have never been guilty of so many unbecoming and disgraceful actions as this man. The only person for whom he ever interested himself was a Count Aceto, the most notorious gambler and profligate, who had been expelled from the Tuscan and the Lucca States. And now his conscience will not permit him to sanction a father's disposal of his daughter in marriage with almost the only man who deserves her, and certainly the very man who deserves her most.

' I said little in reply to Lord B., only to praise his coolness and forbearance. Nothing can be wiser than the resolution, to consider in the light of diplomacy what has happened, or more necessary than to represent it, in all its circumstances to the Administration at home; without which it cannot fail to be misinterpreted here, whatever care -and anxiety the friends of your family may display, in setting right the erroneous and malicious. I hope Count D'Orsay sees the affair in the same point of view as I do, and will allow his resentment to lose itself among feelings more congenial to him. Lord B., I do assure your ladyship, has quite recovered his composure : I hope that you have too—otherwise the first smile on seeing him at Rome will not sufficiently reward him for his firmness and his judgment.

'With every good wish in all its intensity to the .happy couple, and with one good wish of much the same nature to Miss Power,—I remain your ladyship's very devoted servant.'

The Blessingtons therefore left Florence, as already stated, and arrived in Rome in November 1827, *en route* for Naples, where, according to the Annual Register, the marriage of Lady Harriet Gardiner and Count Alfred D'Orsay was celebrated by the chaplain to the British Embassy. The family then returned to Rome, from where four days later the bridegroom addressed the following letter concerning the arrangements, to Landor :—

'Rome, *Decembre* 8, 1827.

'Mon Cher Mr Landor,—Nous avons tous été obligè d'aller à Naples pour faire le mariage Protestant, car la première insinuation qu'a l'on

donna au Duc de Laval, fut qu'il étoit préférable
que cela eut lieu avant la cérémonie Catholique,
ainsi voila ce grand imbecille d'un ministre con-
fondu. Son ignorant entêtement est prouvé. Je
viens de lui écrire, pour lui dire que lors qu'on
est complètement ignorant des devoirs de son
ministère on doit alors en place d'entêtement s'en
rapporter à l'opinion des autres, et que malgré
tout l'embarras que nous avions eu à cause de
lui, d'entreprendre ce voyage, nous avions été à
même de juger de F——, qui comprend tout
aussi, bien les devoirs de son ministère que la
manière de recevoir les personnes de distinction.

'J'espere qu'il prendra mal ma lettre, car
j'aurais grand plaisir de lui couper le bout de
son bec. Je vous écris ces détails car je sais
même par Hare, qu'en veritable ami vous avez
pris chaudement notre parti; je ne m'en étonne
pas, car il suffit de vous connaitre, et de pouvoir
vous apprécier, pour être convaincu que tout ce
qui n'est pas sincere n'a rien de commun avec
vous. Toute la famille vous envoye mille
amitiés, nous parlons et pensons souvent de
vous.—Votre très affectionné, D'ORSAY.'

Whatever the intentions of the newly-married pair regarding their future home may have been, for the present they lived in the Palazzo Negroni, and from there travelled with Lord and Lady Blessington and Miss Power through Italy into France on their way to England.

Passing through various towns they came at last to Genoa, and here it was that a little incident occurred which shows the thought and kindness of Lady Blessington's disposition ; they being the secret by which she won and held the admiration and affection of all who knew her.

During their first stay in the city she had been attracted by a pretty child whose brown-faced father mended shoes outside his door in a narrow high-housed passage not far from their hotel. This child, the little Teresina, who was but two years old, was the light of her parents' eyes ; and was dearer to them from the fact that already they had lost two children before they had reached her age.

Bright and merry she would dance round

her father, put a flower to his nose, crow with delight and hide behind the apron of her mother, who knitting as she leaned against the door-post, watched the sprite's movements, greedy of happiness. One day Lady Blessington stayed to kiss the child, by which she won its parents' hearts for ever; and after this, whenever she would pass, Teresina would clap her hands for joy, hold out a flower for her to smell, or offer her lips to be kissed: when the father and mother radiant with pride and joy would tell in high-pitched tones of their darling's wonderful intelligence.

Before leaving, the Countess bought some presents, amongst them a silver medal of St Teresa, for the child to whom she bade good-bye: but next morning the father and mother with their little one were waiting outside the hotel to see them off, carrying two bouquets which they presented, their prayers for the foreigners being interrupted by tears.

On returning to Genoa the cobbler and his wife were not in their accustomed place, and nothing was known of them by those now occupying their house. Anxious to see them, Lady Blessington offered a reward to the *laquais-de-place* if he could find them, and eventually they were discovered in a poor quarter of the town where she went to see them. Nothing could equal their gratitude and joy which soon however was turned into tears. The light of their life had gone out, and they could not remain in the old darkened house. And for long they spoke of the sorrow, the mother taking from her neck the medal of which the child had been so proud. Lady Blessington forced some presents upon them and left them with their prayers ringing in her ears.

A more cheerful episode marked the close of this second visit to Genoa. They had bidden farewell to all the well-remembered spots including Byron's palace, and on the morning of their departure, imperials and chaise seats were packed, bills paid, 'canvas sacks of silver given to the courier,' and letters of credit made out, when Lady Blessington was taken to see a charming carriage which had arrived from England, and was similar to one she had admired when in Florence, belonging to the English minister's wife. She praised this highly and was then told it was hers, having been specially ordered and sent from London for her journey.

'Lord Blessington' she says 'has a princely way of bestowing gifts.'

TRAVELLING slowly as was their wont, the
Blessingtons, with the Count and Countess
D'Orsay and Miss Power, reached Paris on a
hot day in June 1828 and took up their residence in the Hôtel de Terrasse, Rue de Rivoli.
Their stay here was but temporary, one of
the first things which occupied them being the
search for a suitable residence. This after some
time was found in a magnificent house which
had once belonged to Maréchal Ney.

This mansion which had been to let but three
days, was taken at an enormous rental by the

Blessingtons, who outbid all competitors. It was situated in the Rue de Bourbon and looked out upon the gardens of the Tuileries and the Seine. Approached by an avenue of trees that ended in a court, it was enclosed from the Rue de Bourbon by high walls, and separated from the Quai d'Orsay by a terrace planted with flowers. From a lofty vestibule opened suites of finely-proportioned rooms with fluted pilasters and chimney-pieces of Parian marble, their walls and ceilings still fresh with decorations that had cost a million francs.

Furniture suitable to this palatial residence was now hired for a year, on condition that should its purchase be desirable after that period, allowance would be made for the hire money. Whilst the house was being prepared Lady Blessington amused herself by visiting it, but was not allowed to see her bed, dressing, or bathrooms until they were finished; this suite being specially decorated and furnished from designs by her husband, who when they were completed took her to see them.

Nothing could exceed the luxury of these

apartments. A silvered bed rested on the back of silver swans 'so exquisitely sculptured that every feather is in *alto relievo* and looks nearly as fleecy as those of the living bird.' Curtains of pale blue silk, carpets of uncut pile, silver lamps, luxurious couches, immense mirrors, and 'a rich coffer for jewels,' completed the arrangements. The bathroom was more beautiful still, with its white marble and its frescoed ceiling representing Flora scattering flowers with one hand, whilst from the other was suspended an alabaster lamp in the shape of a lotus.

'The whole fitting up is in exquisite taste' she writes 'and as usual, when my most gallant of all gallant husbands that it ever fell to the happy lot of woman to possess, interferes, no expense has been spared. A queen could desire nothing better for her own private apartments. Few queens, most probably, ever had such tasteful ones.'

On the day before they moved into their new residence, June 14th, Lord Blessington wrote to Landor telling him of their intended change, and stating that Lady Blessington wished that some whim, caprice, or other impelling power might transport him across the Alps, and give them the pleasure of again seeing him.

'Here we have been nearly five weeks' he tells his correspondent 'and unlike to Italy and its suns, we have no remembrance of the former, but in the rolling of the thunder; and when we see the latter, we espy at the same time the threatening clouds on the horizon. To balance or assist such pleasure we have an apartment *bien decoré* with *Jardin de Tuileries en face*, and our apartment being at the corner, we have the double advantage of all the *row* from morning till night. Diligences and *fiacres*—coachmen cracking their whips, stallions neighing, carts with empty wine barrels—all sorts of discordant music, and all kinds of cries, songs, and the jingling of bells. But we hope this is our last day of purgatory: for though the skies are loaded with more water than one could expect —after so much pouring, yet midst thunder, lightning, and rain, we are to strike our tents and march.'

A staff of domestics including a groom of the
chambers, a *maître d'hôtel*, and a cook who was
'an inimitable artist' was added to the servants
who had travelled with the family. Once settled
in their new home the Blessingtons began to
entertain with their usual sumptuous hospitality.
A vast number of guests, foreign princes and
princesses, dukes and duchesses, counts and
countesses, English ambassadors and men of
title, were bidden to dinners, breakfasts, and
suppers; the host and hostess being entertained in return. A glittering gaiety
seemed the order of the day. Now they are
in their box at the opera witnessing the *début*
of Taglioni who has introduced a new style of
dancing, 'graceful beyond all comparison, wonderful lightness, an absence of all violent effort,
and a modesty as new as it is delightful to
witness in her art.' Again they attend a
grand review in the Champ de Mars at which
Charles X., the dauphin, dauphine, and the
Duchesse de Berri were present; Lady
Blessington chaperoned by the Duchesse
de Guiche, sitting beside the Marchioness de

Loulé sister to the King of Portugal, in the front row of the grand pavilion.

All things seemed to prosper with Lady Blessington ; and amongst other pleasant events came the marriage of her sister Ellen, Mrs Purves, to the Right Honourable John Manners Sutton, afterwards Viscount Canterbury, which was celebrated on the 6th of December 1828. Mr Manners Sutton had been a widower since 1815, whilst Mrs Purves had been a widow since the 27th of September 1827, her husband having died on that date at Pensacola where he had for four years held the post of British Consul. Amongst the letters of congratulation which Lady Blessington received on this marriage was the following from her friend Landor :—

' Fortune is not often too kind to me—indeed why should she be, but when she is, it is reasonable enough I should be grateful. We have come at last to this agreement, that whenever she does anything pleasant to you, I may take my part in the pleasure, *nem. con.*, and as large a part as anyone except yourself and Lord B.

She then put something into the opposite scale, and said it was but just. I laughed to hear her talk of justice, but owned it. Now I will lay a wager that, of the hundreds of letters you and my lord have received to congratulate you on the marriage of Mrs Purves, not one has been so long in coming to the point. . . .

'I am waiting very anxiously to offer Miss Power better compliments than these of the season. Why is she contented with holly, when she may have myrtle? I must not begin to ponder and meditate, for whatever effect these ponderings and meditations may have upon the ponderer and meditator, the effect is likely to be very different on those whom they befall. And I do not think your post comes in at bedtime. I have not yet transgressed so far, that I may not request to be presented to all your house, and to wish you many many years of health and happiness.'

A month before this event took place Lady Blessington received a letter from her old friend Tom Moore who was then engaged in writing his life of Byron. Moore had heard from Lord John Russell that she had seen a good deal of Byron during his last days in Italy, that she could narrate many anecdotes of him, and that she possessed some verses addressed to herself by the poet. 'Now my dear Lady Blessington' wrote Moore insinuatingly, 'if you have anything like the same cordial remembrances of old times that I have—if ever the poet (or the piper) found favour in your ears, sit down instantly and record for me as only a woman *can* record, every particular of your acquaintance with Byron from first to last. Above all do not forget the verses, which will be doubly precious as written *by him* on *you.*'

Lady Blessington ever anxious to help or to please her friends, readily complied with his request, and to her is due the interesting particulars the biographer gives of Byron's last days in Genoa. When the book was published however she was not forwarded a presentation copy, 'all owing to a mistake, or rather a difficulty in the way of business' as Moore wrote to explain when reminded of his want of courtesy. 'It is too long a story for a man in a hurry to relate, but you will understand enough, when I tell you that the dispensation of the presentation copies was a joint concern between Murray and me, and that having by mistake exceeded my number, I was unwilling to embarrass my account by going further.

'But mind whatever copy you may have *read* me in, the one you must go to *sleep upon* (when inclined for a doze) must be a portable octavo presented by myself. You deserve ten times more than this, not only for your old friendship, but for the use you have been to the said volumes by the very interesting and (in the present state of the patrimonial question) *apropos* contributions you have furnished.'

The year 1829 did not begin propitiously for Lady Blessington; her health became uncertain, she was subject to depression. Writing to Landor in February she begs that he will not think her ungrateful for not answering his last letter 'but when I tell you' she says 'that for the last two months I have only twice attempted to use my pen, and both times was compelled to abandon it, you will acquit me of neglect or negligence, neither of which, towards those whom I esteem and value as highly as I do you, are among the catalogue of my faults. The change of climate, operating on a constitution none of the strongest, and an unusually severe winter, to me, who for years have only seen Italian ones, has brought on a severe attack of rheumatism in the head, that has not only precluded the possibility of writing, but nearly of reading also.'

It was a couple of months later, during which she felt little better, that her husband received from Lord Rosslyn who acted as whip for his party, the following letter relative to the Catholic Emancipation Bill, which was then agitating the United Kingdom :—

' Knowing the deep interest you have always taken in the peace and prosperity of Ireland, and the anxious zeal with which you have upon every occasion exerted yourself in favour of the repeal of the civil disabilities upon the Catholics, I take the earliest opportunity of apprising you of the present situation of that question.

' It has become of the utmost consequence to

obtain the best attendance of the friends of civil and religious liberty, in order to give all possible support to the measure proposed by the Duke of Wellington.

' I am persuaded that you will feel with me that the present is a crisis that calls for every possible exertion and sacrifice from those who have as strong feelings and as deep a stake in the peace and prosperity of Ireland as you have ; and you cannot fail to be aware that the object of the Orange and Brunswick Clubs in both countries is to defeat the salutary measures proposed by the Duke of Wellington, and consequently to endanger the security of all property in Ireland and the peace of the Empire.

' If you see this subject in the same light that I do, you will not hesitate to come over to take your seat ; and I should venture to suggest to your lordship, if that should be your determination, that you should come before the second reading of the Bill, and remain till after the Committee ; and if you will do me the honour to signify your commands to me, I will take care to give you timely notice of the day on which it may be necessary for you to be in the House of Lords for the purpose of taking the oaths, and will take charge of seeing that your writ is ready.'

Though Lord Blessington was not quite well at this time, and though the journey from the French to the English capital was tedious and uncomfortable, he resolved to cross the Channel and be in his place in the House of Peers when the bill came up for discussion; for my Lord was a liberal man in his ideas, and had ever been a lover of his country. Lady Blessington writes that he never considered himself, when a duty was to be performed. She adds, ' I wish the question was carried and he safely back again. What would our political friends say if they knew how strongly I urged him not to go, but to send his proxy to Lord Rosslyn?'

His journey seemed to have no ill results, for when in London he appeared in excellent spirits and good health. He voted for the Catholic Emancipation Bill, which was passed by a majority of one hundred and five; saw many of his friends and entertained them in St James's Square; dined with Lord Rosslyn; and at the request of the Duke of Clarence, presided at the Covent Garden theatrical fund dinner. He then set out again for France where he was joyously welcomed by his wife, his daughter, and his son-in-law. Always lavishly generous to the woman he loved, he came back to her laden with presents. 'Some of them' she writes 'are quite beautiful and would excite the envy of half my sex.'

Lord Blessington had been generally careful of his health, but for years had suffered from gout, was susceptible to cold, and had a horror of draughts. D'Orsay used laughingly to tell the Earl he could detect a current of air caused by the key being left crossways in the keyhole of a door.

Charles Mathews tells an anecdote of being with him and Lady Blessington when they went on an exploring expedition to Baiæ, where was an old Roman villa whose foundations extended out into the bay, whilst portions of its walls rose about two or three feet above the water.

On these young Mathews skipped about at his pleasure, when to his surprise Lord Blessington called out 'Take care, take care, for heaven's sake mind what you are about : you'll be in the water to a certainty.'

Mathews took no heed, on which the warning was repeated greatly to his surprise, for my lord had little fear of danger for himself or others ; when Lady Blessington begged he would let the boy alone. 'If he does fall into the water what can it matter?' she asked. 'You know he swims like a fish.'

'Yes, yes' answered the Earl 'that's all very well, but I shall catch my death driving home in the carriage with him.'

At the time when danger was nearest to him it was least feared. Paris was looking at its best and brightest one day soon after his return from London, the purity of spring and the promise of summer in the air, the sky clear for the sun, and the city gay with colour, all on this May day which was to be the last but one for this most devoted of husbands, this generous-hearted, open-handed, pleasure-loving man; than whom as Walter Savage Landor wrote, 'none was ever dearer or more delightful to his friends.'

It was on a Saturday the 23d of the month that soon after the mid-day meal he complained of not feeling well ; when he drank a few spoonfuls of Eau de Melisse in water. An hour or so later, feeling much better he ordered his horse, and followed by his servant rode out of the courtyard of his house, a gallant upright figure, his sunny high-coloured face turned towards the window from which his wife watched him, he waving his hand in response to her smiles.

A little later and he was carried home insensible from an attack of apoplexy. Doctors were hastily summoned, and all that love could do was done ; the knowledge of its helplessness being in such cases love's bitterest grief. From the first he remained speechless and insensible, his wife distracted and fearful beside him, servants coming and going, his daughter and her husband seldom absent from the room over which the sombreness of death seemed already to have settled. All through Sunday, a day of sunshine and joyousness without, of grief and terror within, his condition remained unchanged: but on Monday morning at half-past four the stertorous breathing ceased, and those around were forced to recognise that he was gone. In this way did Charles James first Earl of Blessington die in the forty-sixth year of his age.

'Nothing can equal the grief of poor Lady Blessington' writes her sister to Landor. 'In fact she is so ill that we are quite uneasy about her, and so is also poor Lady Harriet. But not only ourselves but all our friends are in the greatest affliction since this melancholy event. Fancy what a dreadful blow it is to us all to lose him; he who was so kind, so generous, so truly good a man.'

By this unforeseen event his wife was deprived of the man who had raised her from dependence and obscurity to rank and fortune, whose will was hers, whose life was devoted to her. In every way her loss was irreparable and she mourned him bitterly. Their many friends wrote messages of sympathy which at such a time had little power to touch the wound with healing. Amongst all she received, those written by Landor, appealed to her most. In a letter dated the 6th of June he writes to her :—

'If I defer it any longer, I know not how or when I shall be able to fulfil so melancholy a duty. The whole of this day I have spent in that stupid depression which some may feel without a great calamity, and which others can never feel at all. Everyone that knows me knows the sentiments I bore towards that disinterested and upright and kind-hearted man, than whom none was ever dearer or more delightful to his friends. If to be condoled with by many, if to be esteemed and beloved by all whom you have admitted to your society is any comfort, that comfort at least is yours. I know how inadequate it must be at such a moment, but I know too that the sentiment will survive when the bitterness of sorrow shall have past away.

'You know how many have had reason to

speak of you with gratitude, and all speak in
admiration of your generous and gentle heart,
incapable as they are of estimating the elevation of your mind.

'Among the last letters I received, was one
from Mrs Dashwood, whose sister married poor
Reginald Heber, the late Bishop of Calcutta.
She is a cousin of Hare's, and has heard
Augustus speak of you as I have often written.
Her words are (if she speaks of faults, remember
you are both women), "I wish I was intimate
with her, for, whatever may be her faults, so
many virtues can be told of few."

'These are the expressions of a woman who
has seen and lived amongst whatever is best
and most brilliant, and whose judgment is as
sound as her heart, and does she not speak
of introduction merely, but of intimacy; it is
neither her curiosity nor her pride that seeks
the gratification.

'I fear that the recovery of your health may
yet be retarded, about which I have often
thought of writing to Count D'Orsay, for nothing
is more inconsiderate than to oppress with a

weight of letters one whom you know to suffer, and to be more than enough fatigued already. May he and his Countess endeavour to promote your happiness as anxiously as you have promoted theirs!

'Believe me, dear Lady Blessington, your very faithful and devoted serv^t.'

And the following month he writes to her on the same subject :—

'DEAR LADY BLESSINGTON,—Too well was I aware how great my pain must be in reading your letter. So many hopes are torn away from us by this unexpected and most cruel blow. I cannot part with the one of which the greatness and the justness of your grief almost deprives me—that you will recover your health and spirits. If they could return at once, or very soon, you would be unworthy of that love which the kindest and best of human beings lavished on you. Longer life was not necessary for him to estimate your affection for him, and those graces of soul which your beauty, in its brightest day, but faintly shadowed. He told me that you were requisite to his happiness, and that he could not live without you. Suppose then he had survived you—his departure, in that case, could not have been so easy as it was, so unconscious of pain—of giving it, or leaving it behind. I would most wish such a temper and soul as his, and next to them such a dissolution. Tho' my hand and my whole body shakes as I am writing it, yet I am writing the truth. Its suddenness—the thing most desirable—is the thing that most shocks us. I am comforted at the reflection that so gentle a heart received no affliction from the anguish and despair of those he loved. You have often brought me over to your opinion after an obstinate rather than a powerful contest ; let me, now I am more in the right, bring you over by degrees to mine, and believe me, dear Lady Blessington, your ever devoted servant.'

The Earl's death had been so sudden, so unforeseen, that its shock and pain were the more terrible to one who owed him an inestimable debt of love and gratitude which it had been her highest happiness to repay. Since her marriage her life had been so full of pleasure that this quick succeeding grief was intolerable. The world seemed completely changed for her. And as in all sensitive natures the strength of the body depends on the condition of the mind, her health gave way and caused much anxiety to those around.

The state of her feelings will be best understood when the following letter written two months after her loss, to Mrs Charles Mathews, is read :—

'I thank you for your kind letter' she begins 'and feel deeply sensible of the sympathy of you and your excellent family, under the cruel and heavy blow that has fallen on me in the loss of the best of husbands and of men ; these are not mere words of course, as all who knew him will bear witness, for never did so kind or gentle a heart inhabit a human form ; and I feel this dreadful blow with even more bitterness, because it appears to me, that while I possessed the inestimable blessing I have lost, I was not to the full extent sensible of its value; while now all his many virtues and good qualities rise up every moment in memory, and I would give worlds to pass over again the years that can never return.

'Had I been prepared for this dreadful event by any previous illness, I might perhaps have borne up against it: but falling on me like some dreadful storm, it has for ever struck at the root of my peace of mind, and rendered all the future a blank. It is not whilst those to whom we are attached are around us in the enjoyment of health and the prospect of a long life, that we can judge of the extent of our feelings towards them, or how necessary they are to our existence. We are God help us, too apt to underrate the good we have, and to see the little defects to which even the most faultless are subject : while their good qualities are not remembered as they ought to be, until some cruel blow like that which has blighted me, draws the veil from our eyes, and every virtue, every proof of affection, are remembered with anguish, while every defect is forgotten.

'What renders my feelings still more bitter is, that during the last few years my health has been so bad, and violent attacks in my head so frequent, that I allowed my mind to be too much engrossed by my own selfish feelings, and an idea of my poor dear and ever-to-be-lamented husband being snatched away before me, never could have been contemplated.

'Alas, he who was in perfect health, and whose life was so precious and so valuable to so many, is in one fatal day torn from me for ever, while I, who believed my days numbered am left to drag on a life I now feel a burden.

'Excuse my writing to you in this strain: I would not appear unkind or ungrateful in not answering your letters, and my feelings are too bitter to prevent my writing in any other.'

In a letter penned more than five years after her husband's death, a date which it may be well to bear in mind, she gives expression to her feelings regarding him, in a letter addressed to Landor. In this, bearing date July 1834 she says :—

'I have often wished that you would note down for me your reminiscences of your friendship and the conversations it led to with my dear and ever-to-be-lamented husband : he who so valued and loved you, and was so little understood by the common herd of mankind. We who knew the nobleness, the generosity, and the refined delicacy of his nature, can render justice to his memory, and I wish that posterity through your means should know him as he was. All that I could say would be viewed as the partiality of a wife, but a friend and such a friend as you, might convey a true sketch of him.'

And now began a time of change and trouble for one whose ways had previously been made smooth by every means that luxury and love could suggest. For in the first place through the death of her lord her circumstances underwent a change, as indeed they must have done had he lived, owing to his vast expenditure, his disregard for money, his neglect of his property which had become heavily encumbered. According to his last will and testament he left her two thousand a year inclusive of one thousand pounds settled on her at the time of his marriage; 'with all her own jewels, requesting that she may divide my late wife's jewels between my two daughters at the time of her decease'; all his carriages, parapher-nalia and plate; and the lease of the house in St James's Square, at the expiration of which the furniture, books etc. were to be moved to his residence at Mountjoy Forest. It may also be mentioned here that he left a thousand pounds each to Robert and to Mary Anne Power.

To one living in the splendour to which she had been accustomed for the past ten years, an annuity of two thousand a year seemed small. But this was not all. Within four months of her husband's death, at a time that she was suffering mentally and physically, and before Count D'Orsay was separated from his wife, the report of a scandal was heard which con-nected his name with Lady Blessington; a scandal which first found voice in a scurrilous London newspaper called the *Age*.

This was a paper which in no ways relied for its circulation on the intelligence of the day but rather on its slanderous attacks on individuals. It was started in 1828 and had for its first editor one Richards, who soon gave place to the notorious Westmacott. Tory in its politics it especially assailed the characters of those who differed from its political opinions. It was not however public men alone, but private individuals, women as well as men, generally those of high social standing, against whom it made the gravest charges.

This paper was rivalled but not equalled in vileness by the *Satirist*, whose province it was to defame all connected with the Tory party; so that between those pests no man or woman was safe. Calumnies were their stock-in-trade; to traduce was their delight.

It is humiliating to human nature to have to relate that these journals were largely indebted for the foul reports they published, to individuals —chiefly women—who from motives of personal malice desired to ruin those they traduced and to whom they openly professed friendship, as was proved. There was one means however of escape, and that was by paying the heavy demands of the blackmailer: for the editors of these villainous papers were in the habit of writing to their intended victims, telling them that certain grave charges had been made against them, and intimating that they were aware of facts more grievous still, particulars of which were for the present withheld, but all of which would be published if within a certain date a specified sum was not forthcoming. If this were paid, they need have no uneasiness; the unpleasant matter referred to would never see the light.

From the fact that many innocent but pusill-animous persons paid the money demanded rather than have their reputations blasted; as well as from the second fact that these papers small in size and published at sevenpence a number had each a circulation of about nine thousand copies a week, it will be seen that the proprietors prospered; their respective in-comes reaching about six thousand a year.

Though some of the maligned were pleased to suffer in silence, in the hope of being able to live down the scandals circulated about them

in these papers, there were others more courageous who sought justice in the law courts, or
satisfaction by personal punishment of the
editors. Actions for libel were therefore continually taken and heavy damages awarded to
the injured; but the publicity which the
journals received at such times, but served as
advertisements which increased their circulation ; so that the charges for advertisements
were raised.

Lord Alfred Paget was to his credit one of
the courageous sufferers who sought redress
from the law. He had been charged by the
Age with striving to extort money from Lord
Cardigan by accusing him of improper intercourse with Lady Alfred. The plaintiff swore
that the conductors of the *Age* had already
threatened that if he did not remit them a
certain sum, they would publish private facts
in their possession regarding the Paget family,
a sum which he had paid.

Those who sought to punish the editors were
not in general so successful as those who appealed to the law ; for it was the practice of

these papers to have in their employ an individual of Herculean proportions, generally a Hibernian of the brutal type, who on the editor being inquired for, stepped forward bludgeon in hand, and declaring himself to be that individual, demanded with a grim smile what his visitor might be pleased to want. That such a condition of tyranny, 'the greatest under the sun,' as the Lord Chief Justice who tried one of the libel cases stated, was suffered for years, seems extraordinary: but it is more wonderful still that the chief offender Westmacott was received by a company of decent men.

Such however was the case: for James Grant says that soon after coming to London he dined at Willis's Rooms on a public occasion when to his surprise he found the editor and proprietor of the *Age* amongst the company, and learned that his name had previously figured in the list of stewards, most of whom were dukes, marquises, and earls, chiefly belonging to the Tory party. 'And at the dinner' he says 'no man played a more prominent part than he. Was it not lamentable to see all the

principles alike of honour and morality sacrificed, as was the case in this instance, to the
exigencies of party ? '

This was the editor in whose paper appeared
the insinuations against Lady Blessington's
reputation ; insinuations which were repeated
by the thoughtless and malicious, from the
effects of which she was never able to rid
herself.

As may be surmised this filth was flung at
her from behind the shelter of an anonymous
name. In a letter dated Paris 24th of September
1829, and signed ' Otiosus,' the writer after mentioning various people, women as well as men, in
a flippant, impertinent, or injurious way, goes on
to say ' Alfred D'Orsay with his pretty pink and
white face drives about *à la* Petersham with a
cocked-up hat and a long-tailed cream-coloured
horse. He says he will have seventeen thousand
a year to spend, others say seventeen hundred :
he and my lady go on as usual.'

In a second letter dated October 5th the same
writer ventures still further in his scandalous insinuations. ' What, a *ménage* is that of Lady

Blessington' he says. ' It would create strange
sensations were it not for one fair flower that still
blooms under the shade of the Upas. Can it be
conceived in England that Mr Alfred D'Orsay
has publicly detailed to what degree he carries
his apathy for his pretty interesting wife. This
young gentleman, Lady Blessington, and the
virgin wife of sweet sixteen all live together.'

Shocked and grieved by such insinuations,
Lady Blessington wrote to Mr Powell the solici-
tor and friend of her late husband, instructing him
to take proceedings against the paper. Probably
he did not consider that the letters, containing
subtle insinuations rather than definite charges,
were actionable ; at all events in the following
December Lady Blessington writes to a friend
complaining that nothing as yet has been done
' either in discovering the author of the scandalous attacks against me, or in preventing a
renewal of them.'

Later she heard that an acquaintance of
theirs a certain Colonel C—— was the writer
of the scandal, and when next she saw him she
charged him with the offence, as will be seen

by the following letter, written to Mrs Charles Mathews :—

'All that has occurred on the subject of the attacks in the *Age*, I shall now lay before you. I wrote to Mr Powell urging him to commence a prosecution against the editor and stated to him that Lord Stuart de Rothsay had advised me to do so, as the only means of putting a stop to these attacks. Mr Powell was of a different opinion, and advised our treating the attack with contempt; and so the affair ended.

'When Colonel C—— returned to Paris in February and came to see me, I told him of my information as to his being the author of the attacks ; but this I did without ever even hinting at my informant. He declared his innocence in the most positive terms, gave his word of honour that he had never written a line in his life of scandal for any paper, and never could lend himself to so base and vile a proceeding. His manner of denial was most convincing, and so it ended.

'Two months ago Captain G—— of the Guards who had been very severely attacked in the *Age*

went to London and took a friend with him to the
Editor of the *Age*, who even gave him a small
piece of the letter sent from Paris, which Captain G—— sent Comte D'Orsay, and which is
a totally different writing from Colonel C——'s :
and so here ended the business, as it was useless to do anything more except commence a
prosecution which I still think ought to have
been done.

'Mr Powell has never given either Comte
D'Orsay or myself the least information since
last January on this subject ; and now you know
all that I do on this point. I have never seen
a single number of the *Age*, do not know a
single person who takes it in, and never hear
it named, so that I am in total ignorance as to
the attacks it contains.'

This scandalous report seems to have had
little effect upon her friends, for not only did
the distinguished foreigners with whom she was
already intimate continue to gather round her,
but English acquaintances passing through or
visiting Paris, made certain to call upon her.
Amongst them such men as Lord John Russell,

Samuel Rogers, the Duke of Hamilton, Lords Palmerston, Castlereagh, Pembroke, and Cadogan, who delighted to converse with her.

Moreover, her step-daughter, known as Lady Mary, visited and remained with her three weeks; the girl feeling the charm of her personality which all who approached Lady Blessington were quick to acknowledge. 'She is all that is most perfect' the latter writes of her step-daughter 'her dear father's kind, noble, and generous heart, with a manner the most captivating: I adore her, and I believe she loves me as few girls can love a mother.'

She now became occupied with business matters in connection with her husband's property which was in some confusion; and the inconvenience of remaining in Paris became evident. Still she was reluctant to leave the French capital and in a letter to Mrs Charles Mathews dated October 1829 she expresses her dislike of returning to England, and declares that business alone could persuade her to settle in London 'for death' she adds 'has deprived me of the friend who could have

rendered my visit there as happy and pros-
perous as all my days were when he lived.
The contrast between the past and the present
would and will be most poignant, but should
our affairs require it I shall certainly go.'

And two months later she says she is still ill
in mind and body and unequal to the exertion
of writing. 'Indeed my health suffers so much
that I fear I shall be obliged to give up residing
at Paris, and be compelled to try the effects of
English air: and this will be very painful to
me, after having gone to so much expense and
trouble in arranging my rooms here, where I am
so comfortably lodged, besides which a residence in England under my present circumstances would be so different to all that I have
been accustomed to, that I cannot contemplate
it without pain. But after all, without health
there is no enjoyment of even the quiet and
sober nature which I seek—a cheerful fireside
with a friend or two to enliven it, or what is
still perhaps more easily had, a good book.
I have never had a day's health since I have
been in France: and though I do all that

I am advised, I get worse rather than better.'

Towards the end of this year her spirits seem to have fallen to a low ebb, and she evidently suffered keenly from depression.

Writing to a friend from Paris, November 30, 1829 she says mournfully enough that her correspondent is one of the few who do not quite forget her: that she has experienced much ingratitude and unkindness which added to the heavy blow that had fallen on her made her dread lest she should become a misanthrope and her heart shut itself against the world.

'If you knew' she adds 'the bitter feelings the treatment I have met with has excited in my breast, you would not wonder that it has frozen the genial current of life, and that I look as I am, more of another world than this. Had God spared me my ever dear and lamented husband, I could have borne up against the unkindness and ingratitude of friends estranged : but as it is the blow has been too heavy for me, and I look in vain on every side for consolation.

'I am wrong my dearest in writing to you in

this gloomy mood, but if I waited until I became more cheerful, God alone knows when your letter would be answered. You are young and life is all before you, take example by me and conquer while yet you may, tenderness of heart and susceptibility of feeling which only tend to make the person who possesses them wretched ; ·for be assured you will meet but few capable of understanding or appreciating such feelings, and you will become the dupe of the cold and heartless, who contemn what they cannot understand, and repay with ingratitude the affection lavished on them.

'I would not thus advise you, if I did not know that you had genius; and whoever had that fatal gift without its attendant malady, susceptibility and deep feeling, which in spite of all mental endowments render their possessor dependent on others for their happiness : for it may appear a paradox, but it is nevertheless true, those who are most endowed can the least suffice for their own happiness.'

For months she hesitated about leaving Paris. In May 1830 she writes that she can name

no definite period for her return to England;
'pecuniary affairs prevent me at present, though
I am anxious to go, in the hope that change of
air may do me good, my health and spirits
being very, very poorly. This month as your
heart may tell you, is a great trial to me; it has
renewed my grief with a vividness that you
can understand: for it is dreadful to see all
nature blooming around, and to think that the
last time I welcomed the approach of spring,
I was as happy as heart could wish, blessed
with the best and most delicate of friends, while
now all around me wears the same aspect, and
all within my heart is blighted for ever.'

It was not until November 1830 that she
left Paris. When the day came for her to bid
farewell to her friends she quite broke down,
foreseeing that she would never meet many of
them again.

'Adieu Paris' she writes in her diary 'Two
years and a half ago I entered you with glad-
ness, and the future looked bright; I leave you
with altered feelings, for the present is cheer-
less and the future clouded.'

CHAPTER IX

IN November 1830 Lady Blessington with
her sister Miss Power and the Count and
Countess D'Orsay returned to London and
took up their residence in St James's Square.
Their stay here however was not for long.
It will be remembered that according to the
late Earl's will, his wife was left this residence
until its lease expired, when its furniture and
belongings were to be removed to Mountjoy
Forest. To maintain so large an establishment was an expense which Lady Blessington
with her dowry of merely two thousand

a year, could not afford: and as she had brought with her from abroad a quantity of beautiful cabinets, tables, and other furniture, together with carpets, pictures, china, ornaments, and various objects of art, she resolved to sell her interest in the remaining years of the lease, and rent a smaller house for which she already had almost sufficient furniture.

Though she sanctioned and enjoyed the lavish expenditure in which her husband's princely income allowed him to indulge; from this time forward, without depriving herself of the splendour which had become necessary to her enjoyment, she became an excellent manager, who systematically kept her accounts and sought to control her outlay. Her first movement now was to let the St James's Square mansion which was rented furnished by the Windham Club for thirteen hundred and fifty pounds per annum; but as the head rent was eight hundred and forty pounds a year, this did not add much to her income; especially as she was being continually worried by claims for repairs of the house which was much dilapidated. She therefore eventually sold her interest in it to the executors of Lord Blessington's will.

From St James's Square she moved to a house in Seamore Place which, decorated from designs by D'Orsay and furnished according to her taste, became as Disraeli said 'the most charming of modern houses.' Its library was long and narrow, with deep windows looking out upon Hyde Park, its walls of white and gold were well nigh covered with handsomely bound volumes, above whose cases stood royal blue vases that had once belonged to Marie Antoinette and porcelain bowls on whose purple surface glittered the Imperial cipher. Etruscan tripods stood in its corners; in its recesses were desks of red tortoise-shell boule work. The drawing-room with its deep rich tones of ruby and gold, was not less splendid. Here were turquoise and Sèvres-topped tables, old boule-winged cabinets, antique jugs of flawless amber that had belonged to Josephine, Indian jars, porcelain essence burners, candelabra of jasper and filagree gold, and a thousand other objects that dazzled and delighted the sight.

Jekyll writing to a friend described the house as 'a *bijou*, or, as Sir W. Curtis' lady said a perfect *bougie*.' Little wonder that Sir William Gell writing from Naples says, that Keppel Craven tells him, her house ' is so exquisite in all respects that he thinks it impossible anything can ever tempt you to move again.'

Altogether Lady Blessington made her home a stately and beautiful place worthy of the bright company that was to gather there and become associated with her name for ever. For no sooner had she settled in London than the friends who had been introduced to her by her husband, as well as many of those she had met abroad, mindful of the charm of her personality, grateful for the kindness she had extended to them, hastened to .pay her their court : all of them anxious again to expand their minds in the atmosphere of one so sympathetic and gracious, so graceful and beautiful.

The noblest men in the land, ministers, ambassadors, and politicians ; great artists such as Sir Edwin Landseer, Sir Michael Archer Shee, David Wilkie, Sir Francis Grant, Maclise, and Mulready ; famous poets such as Moore, Rogers, and Campbell ; Indian princes ; generals and diplomatists ; men of various callings and diverse minds all found in her the interest each required in his pursuit, the advice that some requested, the encouragement which others needed ; her exquisite tact guiding her to the knowledge of individual temperament, and prompting the words appropriate to each man's mood ; the natural kindness of her heart and fascination of her personality, binding all to her service, free slaves of a woman they loved.

Never was she seen to such supreme advantage, never were the charms of her personality more persuasive than when seated at the head of her dinner-table surrounded by a brilliant company of friends. Here, resplendent and picturesque, enthroned in a state-chair glowing in crimson and gold, which had been ordered by George IV. for the reception of Louis XVIII. she presided over a feast worthy of her guests.and of herself.

Always sumptuous in her apparel, the rich-hued velvets and sun-gleaming satins she wore, lost in smoothness by contrast with the softness of her rounded throat, the delicate curving breasts, her shoulders, and beautifully shaped arms; with every elegant movement of which her jewels shone as with the splendour of starlight. The wide calm forehead was yet without a line, the exquisite mouth was as mobile and tender as before. The grey-blue eyes whose wistfulness was visible in their depths, whose colour deepened to violet in the shadow of their lids, lighted a face not the less fascinating now it no longer retained the violent freshness of youth ; for time had taught and sorrow had softened, and each in turn had added its tribute to an expression, that more than the shape of feature or the outline of face, was found the chiefest of her charms.

The soothing light of candles fell upon a

table set with a service of chased silver and
old gold, and beautified—after a fashion Lady
Blessington was first to introduce—with the
luxuriant colour of mellow fruits and odorous
flowers in dishes and bowls of sea - green
Sèvres and purple porcelain. The rich amber
or deep ruby of rare and fragrant wines
caught the light of taper flames, whose reflections in the goblet-shaped glasses, gleamed
as might sacred lamps on the altar of
Epicurus. Servants in powder, wearing
magnificent liveries of green and gold walked
silent-footed as if they trod on air, serving
ready-carved—a mode new to England—the
pompous procession of dishes whose insinu-
ating flavour wooed the most reluctant appetite.
And all around, serving as a frame to so
fair a picture, was the superb octagonal-shaped
room in which was empannelled mirrors that
duplicated the lights until they looked innumerable. Those bidden to the enjoyment
of such perfect pleasures, were men whose
talents and achievements were their passports
to the presence of their gracious hostess. In

such company as hers, amidst such scenes as this, the heart kept holiday, the mind was brightest. And so the wittiest sally of Jekyll, the cleverest stories of Lyndhurst and Brougham, the best of Moore's *bon mots*, the worthiest epigram of Rogers, Lord Wellesley's daintiest compliment, were reserved for her ears. Indeed at her table, as Jekyll wrote 'there was wit, fun, epigram, and raillery enough to supply fifty county members for a twelvemonth.'

In all cases the conversation around her board or in her *salon*, was directed rather than led by her; who though a delightful talker and a *raconteuse* without equal, preferred to listen to those who could charm and amuse, and was ever anxious to draw from each his views on the talent which distinguished him most; so that she made all men appear at their best to themselves and to others.

At this date her circle was not enriched by the host of editors, authors, and journalists which it was soon to number when she joined their ranks. Nor in England, were women, her own relatives and a few intimates excepted, found at her table: for in this country the circumstances which preceded her second marriage, were considered to place an insurmountable obstacle to social intercourse with her own sex; a prejudice that was not lessened by the scandalous insinuations of a scurrilous journal, and by an event which soon happened in her domestic circle.

It may however be mentioned here that many of her most intimate friends have stated, that none of those who knew her thoroughly, believed her guilty of the charges of intimacy with Count D'Orsay, made against her by the world at large, which remained ignorant of her real character and of the force of circumstances by which she was beset.

She was not however wholly ostracised by her own sex, for by some bye-law of convention difficult to understand, many women, chiefly belonging to the literary calling, visited her by day, but rigorously excluded themselves from her *salon* at night. On her part

Lady Blessington made it a rule never to accept invitations even when coming from those who called upon her : a sense of dignity counselling her to avoid accidental meeting with those who doubting her position, might wound her susceptibilities.

Therefore on nights when she did not visit the theatre or the opera house, she received at home from eight till twelve, when she enjoyed the conversation of the most intellectual men of the day, who not infrequently gave her their confidence and sought her advice ; in this manner probably compensating for her exclusion from the gossip, scandal, and frivolity indulged in by those of her sex whose virtue debarred them from her presence.

Next to herself the member of her household on whom the inquisitive eyes of the world were most watchfully turned, who with her occupied the chief place in the gossip of society, was Count D'Orsay. On his return to London he was in his thirtieth year, a tall distinguished-looking man with a remarkably graceful figure, clearly cut features, auburn hair and hazel eyes. His manners had the charm and courtesy associated with the courts of France in olden days; his conversation was brilliant in its polished vivacity: his talents were various, and his good-nature was apparent to all. Mrs Newton Crosland whom he once took into dinner, remarked that his hands, large, white, and apparently soft, 'had not the physiognomy which pleases the critical observer and student of hands' for they indicated self-indulgence. She was indeed one of the few who did not admire him; for he struck her observant eyes as being 'mannish rather than manly, and yet with a touch of effeminacy quite different from that woman-like tenderness which adds to the excellence of man.' The many who liked him included Byron, Lamartine, and Landor; and later amongst his warmest friends were Charles Dickens, Captain Marryat, Disraeli and Bulwer; the two last-mentioned authors dedicating each a book to him: whilst John Forster declared the Count's 'pleasantry, wit, and kindliness, gave him a wonderful fascination;' an attestation borne out by Albany Fonblanque who said 'the unique characteristic of D'Orsay is, that the most brilliant wit is uniformly exercised in the most good-natured way. He can be wittier with kindness than the rest of the world with malice.'

Born without a sense of the proportion or value of money, he squandered in reckless extravagance whatever sums came in his way. His wardrobe was inexhaustible, his horses were thoroughbreds, his brougham a work of art, the appointments of his toilet of massive silver and old gold.

Above all things he delighted in emphasising his noble air and distinguished figure by a peculiarity of dress and an exaggeration of fashion which in a man of less remarkable appearance might be considered foppery or affectation. Among other extravagant fancies he suited the shape of his hat to the cut of his coat: donning a hat of smaller dimensions when wearing a thin coat, and of larger size when he wore a thick overcoat or his famous sealskin, which he was the first to introduce to England. In summer he was seen in all the glory of a white coat, blue satin cravat, primrose gloves scented with eau de jasmine, and patent leather boots whose lustre was only second to the sun.

The leader of the dandies, they copied the cut of his garments, the style of his cravats, the fashion of his canes; whilst bootmakers, tailors, and glovers dubbed their wares with his name, as a means of insuring their sale. But though he occupied the unenviable position of a leader of fashion, his talents preserved him from being despised as a fop by his intellectual friends, who however, sometimes good-naturedly bantered him on his splendour. Walter Savage Landor who was anxious that D'Orsay 'should put his pen in motion' wrote to Lady Blessington that he had grown as rich as Rothschild 'and if Count D'Orsay could see me in my new coat, he would not invite me so pressingly to come to London. It would brew ill-blood between us — half plague, half cholera. He would say "I wish that fellow had his red forehead again, the deuce might powder it for him." However as I go out very little I shall not divide the world with him.'

Never perhaps had a man created such a sensation in society as Count D'Orsay. Whether he were guilty or not of the charges which scandal then or afterwards insinuated, was immaterial to those who sought him; save that it lent him a certain piquant interest in the eyes of women who kept apart from Lady Blessington because of her suspected share in his sin: for the noblest hostesses in London gladly opened their doors to him, courted his company, and vied with each other in inviting him to their tables.

He soon became the central figure in a hundred London drawing-rooms, where his epigrams were repeated and his wit was echoed; at Crockford's he gambled for big sums, showing the same good-humoured indifference over his losses as in his gains; at the Coventry he laid down rules regarding sport, on which he was an acknowledged authority; whilst again he flashed into a studio such as Benjamin Haydon's, where he made capital remarks on the picture of the Duke of Wellington the artist was painting, all of which were sound, impressive, and grand 'and must be attended to': and then in a jiffy to illustrate what he meant, in the full pride of his dandyism and without removing his immaculate gloves, 'he took up a nasty oily dirty hogtool' and lowered the hind quarters of Copenhagen the Duke's charger, by bringing over a bit of sky. After that he bounded into his cab like a young Apollo with a fiery Pegasus, as the painter writes, adding quaintly enough 'I looked after him. I like to see such specimens.'

Meanwhile Lady Harriet who was his wife in name only, had grown into a remarkably handsome woman, with finely chiselled features, a delicate complexion, and a distinguished air. In August 1831 she had reached her nineteenth birthday: and had now gained a self-possession, force of will, and power of thought that, had they been hers some four years previously, would have preserved her from a union which was unsuitable and unhappy from the first. Her temperament in all ways differed from D'Orsay's. Brilliant, dashing, and amusing, he saw the world from an exterior point, whilst she in the solitude which she preferred, and because of the wrongs which were hers, had become sensitive and grave, had grown to look beneath the surface of things, and to regard mankind for what they were, rather than for what they seemed.

That her husband who was almost worshipped abroad, neglected one who failed to appreciate him, there can be no doubt; and the injustice of his treatment was emphasised by the fact of all he owed her. For within twelve months of his marriage he received as part of her dowry twenty thousand pounds: whilst Lord Blessington bound his executors, within twelve months of his decease to invest a similar sum in the funds, the interest thereof to be paid to Count D'Orsay during his life, and after his death to his wife Lady Harriet: the principal at her death going to any children of their marriage, or in case of failure of issue, to be held in trust for the executor and administrator of D'Orsay.

Though Lady Blessington extended to her the kindness she showed to all, yet Lady Harriet, young, retiring, and occupying an equivocal position, could not but feel suppressed, and considered herself slighted in the society which gathered round her beautiful and intellectual step-mother. Jekyll in one of his letters to Lady Gertrude Sloane Stanley gives a picture of 'the pretty melancholy Comtesse' gliding into the drawing-room for a few minutes after one of those *Cuisine de Paris exquise* at which she had not been present, and then retiring 'to nurse her influenza.' Instead of being the wife of her husband and the mistress of a home, she found herself a supernumerary in a circle with which she had no sympathy. Disagreements followed, rebellion set in ; and in the autumn of 1831, she and Count D'Orsay separated by mutual consent.

Her subsequent history may be anticipated. Having left Seamore Place, she, accompanied by her aunt and her sister, travelled through Italy and eventually settled in Paris. Here she occupied her time in writing feuilletons and novels in the French language, in the preface to one of which, *L'Ombre du Bonheur*, she says 'Being left alone in the wide world at twenty years of age, without the blessings of a family and without any direct objects to which my affections might be legitimately attached, I soon acquired the habits of contemplation and remark, and as an inevitable consequence that of writing. Silent and reserved it was a constant consolation to me to confine my inmost thoughts to the guardianship of paper, instead of communicating them to those everyday acquaintances, miscalled friends: who too frequently wantonly betray that confidence which has been intrusted to them.'

In Paris she mixed amongst the society to which her rank entitled her. Young and beautiful, unprotected and sympathetic, she was much admired, and eventually she contracted a friendship with the Duc d'Orléans,

prince royal of France and son of Louis
Philippe 'whose sheltering kindness' we are
delicately told 'could not have been otherwise than thankfully received by one in so
desolate and peculiar a situation.'

On Lady's Harriet's departure, the scandal
that before had seemed vague and ill-founded,
now gained strength, and as it would appear
foundation. All kinds of rumours were in the
air. Count D'Orsay could no longer remain
under Lady Blessington's roof, and accordingly
he took a small house in Curzon Street close
by. Neither he nor the Countess seemed to
realise that a return to his own country
was necessary to silence slander. He was
so to speak her son-in-law, a family tie
regarded with more reverence in his country
than in this; she was nearly twelve years
his senior; and moreover shortly before her
death his mother had extracted a promise
from Lady Blessington that she would look
after the Count, who as has already been
stated, was wholly ignorant of the value of
money, and incapable of curtailing his own

extravagances, or of guarding himself against imposition.

At all events Count D'Orsay, though living elsewhere, was constantly in Lady Blessington's house, where it will be remembered her sister Miss Power resided ; he entertaining her guests, and maintaining with her an unbroken friendship ; their manner being, as Mrs Newton Crosland says, 'very much that of mother and son.'

Though secretly humiliated and grieved by the scandal which assailed her, Lady Blessington now more than ever resolved to present a brave front to the world. Accordingly she entertained as before, the distinguished men who remained her friends through life ; and frequently was present in her box at the opera where sumptuously attired and magnificently bejewelled, she was, more than royalty itself, the object on which thousands of eyes were curiously bent, towards which innumerable glasses were turned : she receiving between the acts, as might a queen her courtiers, the most notable members of both houses of parliament, judges, generals, and diplomats who came to pay her in public the tribute of their homage.

And when she drove abroad to take the air, her passage through the streets or round the Row, attracted the wonder and admiration of all who saw: for her carriage 'the most faultless thing of its kind in the world,' resembled a chariot in size. Gracefully built and lightly hung, it was painted green, the wheels white picked out with green and crimson, whilst the panels were emblazoned with arms and supporters, surmounted by a coronet. It was drawn by a splendid pair of dark bays, and driven by a coachman in powdered hair, velvet breeches, and silken stockings, whose elevation on an unusually high box-seat, made him conspicuous above his fellows. The two footmen who stood behind were clad as he, and matched each other in their equal height of six feet.

But all this bravery of appearance did not shield her against the mortifications to which an equivocal position exposed a woman of sensitive mind, whose desire it was to win the amity of all, to incur the malice of none. And guard against them as she might, or ignore them as she would make it appear, there were ever slights and slurs to be met and endured, flung at her in subtle and unexpected ways by her relentless sex, which in secret made her wince.

It was only to those whom she believed were her sincere friends, that she deigned to show her heart. Amongst those she included Mrs Charles Mathews, who since her son had been the guest of the Blessingtons, had continually expressed her gratitude to and friendship for them. Writing to her a few weeks after Lady Harriet's departure, the Countess says 'Your letter found me sinking under all the nervous excitation natural for a sensitive person to feel under such painful and embarrassing circumstances as I find myself placed in.'

And towards the end of this year, December the 7th, 1831, in a letter also addressed to Mrs Mathews, there is a bitter cry that shows how sore was the wound from which she suffered. In this she says—'What shall I say in return for the many sweet but too flattering things your partiality has prompted you to address to me? All that I say is, that if it had been my lot in life to have met with many hearts like yours, I might have become all that your affection leads you to believe me; or if in my near relations I had met with only kind usage or delicacy, I should now not only be a happier, but a better woman, for happiness and goodness are more frequently allied than we think.

'But I confess to you my beloved friend, a great part of the milk and honey of nature with which my heart originally overflowed is turned into gall: and though I have still enough goodness left to prevent its bitterness from falling even on those who have caused it, yet have I not power to prevent its corroding my own heart, and rusting many of the qualities with which nature had blessed me.

'To have a proud spirit with a tender heart

is an unfortunate union, and I have not been able to curb the first or steel the second; and when I have felt myself the dupe of those for whom I sacrificed so much, and in return only asked for affection, it has soured me against a world where I feel alone—misunderstood—with my very best qualities turned against me. If an envious or a jealous crowd misjudge or condemn, a proud spirit can bear up against injustice, conscious of its own rectitude; but if in the most inveterate assailants one finds those whom we believe to be our trusted friends, the blow is incurable and leaves behind a wound that will in spite of every effort, bleed afresh as memory recalls the cruel conduct that inflicted it.

'Cæsar defended himself against his foes, but when he saw his friend Brutus strike at him, he gave up the struggle. If anything can preserve me from the *mildew of the soul* that is growing on me, it will be your affection which almost reconciles me to human nature.'

END OF VOL. I.

Colston and Coy. Limited, Printers, Edinburgh.